AN APOCALYPTIC PLAGUE:
MADE IN THE U.S.A.

Z TOWERS

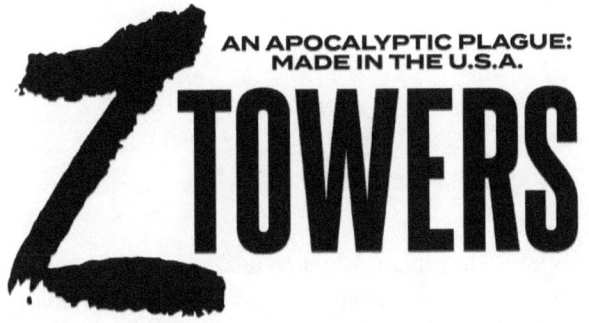

AN APOCALYPTIC PLAGUE:
MADE IN THE U.S.A.

Z TOWERS

JAY ZANO

Copyright © 2017 by Jay Zano
Printed in the United States of America
Contact the author through: JayZano.com
ISBN: 978-0-9987750-0-5

ACKNOWLEDGEMENTS

Thank you to my wife, Jen and son, Tyler for believing in me. You two are my world. I love you both very much!

Thank you to Dan Fazzini for the conversation that started it all.

To Dylan Wininsky, Pete Simons and Tom Wissman, thank you for keeping the story on track by letting me know what worked and more importantly, what didn't.

A special thanks to Robert Wood for your brilliance in editing. The story wouldn't be what it is without your hard work. It was a pleasure working with such a professional.

A quick shout out to Damonza for designing such an awesome book cover.

And finally, A very special and heartfelt thank you to my beautiful wife, Jen. I know I thanked her once already. She told me that she was so supportive of this book she deserved to be thanked twice! I agree.

CHAPTER 1
HOW DID WE GET HERE?

AS WE CRAWL by the executives' posh, windowed conference room, we notice three zombies wearing thousand-dollar suits and shambling about the room like mindless sleepwalkers. That's what they do when they're not ravenous for brains or blood or whatever the hell they sniff out in the living. We've nearly crept by, trying not to catch their lifeless gaze, when Fickle stops dead in his tracks. Suddenly, he stands upright and stares at one of the suits ricocheting away from the corner of the room.

"Hey," he whispers, "isn't that…"

Before either of us can respond, Fick's expression changes from slight fear to an absolute, blind rage.

"Hey, *asshole!*" he screams, whipping the conference room door open. He's spotted Gerry Grand, the building CIO who has made Fickle's life a living hell for the last three years.

"No, Fick, wait," I hiss, but he's already making a beeline for Grand. "Oh shit, let's go!"

With no choice left, we rush in to help. As Fickle closes in, he spots Grand's golf putter leaning against the conference table. He picks it up and, in one fluid motion, hits Grand right across his decomposing jaw. Vegas and I stop for a second, impressed with the fierce blow Fick just dropped on this fool.

"Damn!" we squeal, as Grand flies backwards over the table, but two other zombie-suits are coming our way, and we're forced to refocus quickly. We've actually become quite proficient at killing these things. We weren't always this awesome; our first kills were sloppy; full of fear, hesitation and nausea. Now, we're like badass assassins. Who would have thought a couple of computer guys could be so awesome? We aren't your everyday hero types, blessed with dashing good looks and chiseled physiques. Typically, we're the type of guys who rarely get a second look. However, our societal superpowers of invisibility and obscurity don't apply anymore. We're badass mothers, kicking ass and taking names! I'd like to think that all the endless hours of *Call of Duty* have prepared us for this moment. Anyway, Vegas and I make short work of bludgeoning the other suits.

I stop to confirm my kill, wiping the splattered blood from my face, but I know I can only pause for a brief moment. Vegas and I swing our attention back to Fickle. Vegas moves to help him out, but I hold him back.

"No, let Fick have this. It's been a long time coming."

Grand stumbles back up, his bloody jaw now dangling loosely. Undeterred, he once again lunges in Fickle's direction.

"You never had any intention of giving me that promotion, did you?" Fickle exclaims. "You've made my life miserable for three damn years! Well, payback's a bitch!"

Fick continues to rain blows down on Grand, landing precision shots on each of his extremities. You can hear the snapping of bones in Grand's arms and legs as he's rendered immobile. We find ourselves hollering like we're cheering on a fight at a hockey game.

"Get 'im, Fick!"

"Fuck him up!"

"Yeah!"

Except this isn't a hockey fight, it's our friend pulverizing a zombie with a freaking putter, of all things. I know we're brutal zombie slayers now, but it still feels a little disturbing to be encouraging our friend to kill his boss. That's how far we've come in just a few hours. Not Fick, though. Up until now, Fick had only killed one zombie, and he hasn't really recovered from it. He said he could still see life in Betty when he looked deep into her eyes, like she was trapped inside the monster she had become. After that, he lost his gumption for survival, but we didn't blame him. It's been a mind trip, killing zombies in the afternoon when they were our coworkers this morning. Even the ones I hated were a struggle, in the beginning. Well, Justin and his stupid haircut and desperate attempt to be relevant, I didn't mind that one, but with the rest, it's been a struggle. Even Glen, the loud chip-eater, was a difficult kill for me. Maybe not as hard as it should have been, but still a struggle. That's probably why we're so excited about Fick. Until now, Fickle hasn't been helping us get where we need to be to survive this madness. He's just stood there, sulking, scared and seemingly judgmental while we make all the kills. Maybe this is him turning the corner.

Anyway, as Grand lies on his stomach, disoriented from the repeated blows to his body, Fick raises the putter above his head samurai-style for the kill shot. He slices down at full speed, with that same rage in his eyes, but instead of hearing the sound of the putter blasting through a skull like a shotgun, it sounds much more like he slams it into a sack of tomatoes. Our line of sight obscured by the granite table, we rush over to see the result. Instead of seeing a bashed-to-death Mr. Grand, we see a zombified Mr. Grand squirming on his stomach with a Big Bertha putter hanging right out of his dumb ass.

"How's it feel, you asshole?" Fickle chuckles as he falls back against the wall from pure exhaustion.

"Geez, man," I say, impressed. "You got the whole head up in there! I didn't even think that was possible."

"Wow," Johnny Vegas chimes in, "a hole in one."

I raise my weapon, the trusty ol' blade from an industrial paper cutter, to finish him off. (I did have a better weapon, thanks to Matt, but I've grown partial to this more basic model; made in haste, but it does the job.)

"No!" cries Fickle. "Keep him that way. He deserves to stay a mindless zombie!"

I bet you're wondering how we got here. Well, we're still putting it together ourselves. Today started pretty much like any other day, with us arriving at work at Zook Towers. Johnny Vegas was getting the daily odds on all the office pools, and Fickle was getting his daily dose of abuse from Gerry Grand, who liked to slap Fick around, give him titty-twisters and goose him in the ass with the end of his putter. As for me, I was up to my usual daily duties of fixing computers and making moves on Zoe.

Zoe's the most beautiful woman in the building, and she works on the seventy-fifth floor. I usually spend half my day thinking of ways to run into her 'by chance'. So far, it's only been in the elevator or lobby, but I make the most of it. Speaking of the seventy-fifth, that's the place where all this shit started. It's a locked-down floor dedicated to lab coats, military personnel and lots of top-secret bullshit. The infection started there and spread so fast, too fast for most to react. Anyway we're headed to the top floor now, more or less, in hopes of... Well, let's just get there, first. I've learned not to think too far ahead. One thing is for sure, if we do get out of here alive, I'm going to make some changes; be a better person, live in the moment more. *If* we get out, that is. Maybe Sid was right and there are only two ways out of this godforsaken building: as a mindless zombie or in a body bag. Welcome to Zook Towers!

CHAPTER 2
WELCOME TO ZOOK TOWERS

WALKING UP TO the building is always a mesmerizing experience. Dual hundred-story towers stand side-by-side, connected by two catwalks and an enclosed, external escalator that combine to form a perfect 'Z'; the building's signature look. Tower one has been there for a few years, while tower two is slated to open soon. It'll be a big spectacle, I'm sure. I have to admit, it *is* a breathtaking sight. Coming up to the building, it's always hard not to feel like a celebrity. Tons of tourists can always be found at the base of the buildings, there to get their pictures taken under the 'Z'. There've been plenty of protests held in the same space, thanks to the boss, Mr. Zook, and his constant shady dealings and massive contracts with the military.

Because I work here, I've been asked to pose for pictures on multiple occasions. It seems so ridiculous, but I always oblige, as it's probably as close to celebrity status as I'll ever get. The super-star persona of 'guy who works in the cool building' is always short-lived, and walking in the front doors is enough to remind me that this is my workplace. The job is okay, and the people are cool for the most part; it's Mr. Fredrick J. Zook, billionaire owner of Zook Towers and my boss, that I really can't stand. He represents everything that's wrong with this country: a greedy, self-centered, pretentious, egomaniacal asshole who'd destroy anyone to get what he wants. I guess you could say he's lived the true, rich man's American dream, exploiting everything and everyone to make a profit. He once used eminent domain to close an orphanage so he could put up a mini-mall. He's actually fired people for disagreeing with him or looking at him without permission. He dabbles in everything from franchising ice cream trucks to running a private university where, for the small fee of $75,000, you too can have a 'Zook degree', which is worth about as much as the shit I took this morning.

All of his businesses pale in comparison to his biggest money maker, which is supplying massive amounts of weapons to our military. He's made hundreds of millions, maybe billions, off the backs of tax payers and probably doesn't pay a cent back. He ran for president during the last election cycle, under the brand of fear and idiocy. Almost won, too. He successfully scared a massive amount of Americans, claiming that Mexicans were crossing the border to rape and pillage, the Chinese were stealing our manufacturing jobs and that all Middle Easterners were terrorists here to destroy us. What a disaster it would have been if he'd actually become president. During one of the debates, it came out that the dude thought New Mexico was just a cleaner, rebuilt area in Mexico! He's living proof that you don't have to be smart to be rich. My loathing for this xenophobic asshole washes over me whenever I enter his building, since the entrance has an enormous mural of his big, fat, lumpy head in the lobby for all to see. Being greeted by this obnoxious display of arrogance every day has always pissed me off. He's a squat, chubby little dick with small, peg feet in real life, so it's no surprise that he has this ridiculous mural to convince everyone of how big and powerful he is; it's a hell of a way to overcompensate for his physical and mental shortcomings. I imagine he's got his way his entire life, never having a single person tell him 'no', which is why he feels he can say and do anything he wants without consequence.

*

Zook's Presidential Concession Speech

Hello everyone, and thank you for staying so late. Obviously, this isn't the outcome I, and all of you, were expecting. To be frank, this presidential process is a rigged system designed to help those in power to stay in power. I don't accept the outcome of this election, and cannot endorse Helen Clampton as our next president. She is corrupt and should be in jail. Quite frankly, she's behind all the rigging that's going on in America. So much rigging, folks! It's incredible, absolutely incredible, how much rigging is going on. I have to be honest, folks, she is the main reason why jobs are going to China. She is solely responsible for all the terrorist attacks that have ever happened on American soil, and overseas, and she's the reason why so many Americans are struggling.

Let me tell you, you guys are in for four years of death and destruction in America with Underhand Helen running things. She is a rude old woman who only cares how she can help rich people, illegal immigrants, the gays, the blacks and the corrupt media in this country. So, if you don't fall into one of the categories, guess what? You're screwed! Good luck, folks. You're going to need it.

That said, all is not lost. I, and I alone, will be here to pick up the pieces of this fallen nation and resurrect its days of glory. I first plan on suing America for its rigged system and corrupt media that denied me the presidency by passing false truths about me. So rigged! Then, and here's the most important part, folks, I am opening my own news company called Zook News, where you can get unbiased news from only me and my trusted and loyal sources. Where we will offer you an unfiltered look into the real news that doesn't worry about hurting feelings and political correctness. The true, raw news on how Mexicans are hurting this country, how China is stealing and how the Muslims are all here to take America down. Educate yourselves, folks, because I can't do it alone. Well, I can, but certain laws prohibit me from doing what needs to be done. That's why I needed to be president to do the things that need to be done in this country. You think Underhand Helen can do it? I mean, if she wasn't so old and hadn't already been through menopause, maybe. She could have gotten tough during one of those unpredictable monthly cycles but, without that, she has no fight, no energy in her. I mean, come on folks, does she have the energy and stamina to lead this country? We're all doomed since every other powerful country in this world, and there are a lot of them, folks, will now walk all over us, just like they have been doing for so many years under the previously weak and, quite frankly, pathetic administration.

But I'm going nowhere, folks! I will be here when you need me most. Until then, do your best to arm yourself against the terrorists flooding into this country, the crime that is spiking out of control and the end of America as we know it. Watch Zook News and read my latest book, *Bringing America Back from the Dead* to inform yourselves. God bless you and God bless this nation that used to be the greatest nation on earth. Not anymore, folks, not anymore. Good luck!

*

Besides Zook, it's really not such a bad place to work. Every business you could imagine is in the building. Well, every business that can turn a profit. Each floor offers a different experience; we have floors dedicated to stockbrokers, lawyers, architects, managers, tech development and medical research. Basically, any job you can imagine has a place in this building. I work on the fiftieth floor, which is dedicated to providing tower one with technical support. It's a good job for a couple of reasons. Firstly, we have plenty of work, since most people are absolute bumbling idiots when it comes to pretty much anything that has a plug. Secondly, it's the best job for gossip. No one ever notices the IT guy. Just the other day, I heard Susie got syphilis from Frank, who was also sleeping with Jessica, who's married to a stockbroker on the thirty-eighth floor. It's crazy, like every modern-day soap opera bundled up into real life, and that's even before you consider having complete access to everyone's data. We have terabytes of hard drive space dedicated to all the nude pics we've intercepted from people's computers. Some are truly cringe-worthy! Honestly, it's hard to look some of these people in the eye. I once had a request from a woman known chiefly as a religious zealot to remove all the porn that had 'somehow' ended up on her hard drive. Strangely, she demanded I look at every image with her so we could catalog them for my investigation.

That's the type of job I expect on any given day, and I don't expect anything different this morning. In fact, today starts like most others, with me waiting in line for the Starbucks in our lobby, hoping I can 'run into' Zoe. I can never go see Zoe at work, since the seventy-fifth floor is an off-limits laboratory way above my security clearance. Even IT can't get access; it's *that* locked down. The lobby and the elevator are the only places I ever see her, so I always make sure to make the most of it.

She's so gorgeous; slightly taller than me with dark hair and bright green eyes. I get so mesmerized by her sheer beauty that I can barely conjugate a sentence. Still, I'm hoping that maybe today will be the day that we move on from casual flirting to me actually asking her out on a date.

*

Running into Zoe

"Hello, stranger," I say awkwardly, "fancy meeting you here."

"Yes, fancy meeting you here, in this line where I happen to run into you every day," she says, smiling slightly. "Is this our fourth morning in a row?"

"Well, five if you count Friday of last week," I say blushingly.

"It seems like I have my very own stalker."

"Me, a stalker?" I say, blowing on my latte to seem casual. "Uh, I think we're just on the same schedule."

"A likely story!"

"So, how's work?" I ask, as we get in the elevator.

"You know, same old, same old."

"What is it you do, up on the seventy-fifth?"

"Just stuff," she says, not seeming too comfortable.

"Oh, that's right. Top-secret stuff that you're not allowed to discuss with us common folk."

"Well, I could tell you, but I'd have to kill you," she whispers, smiling.

"I get it. Well, listen, no matter where this goes, your secrets are my secrets and you can trust me."

"'Where this goes'? What, are we dating now?" she asks, confused but playful.

"No, I mean this blossoming friendship," I stammer. "Or, well, if you're interested in taking the next step, I'm not seeing anyone."

The elevator doors open; we've reached the fiftieth floor.

"Isn't this your floor?" she asks.

"Looks like it. To be continued?" I blurt as the door starts to close.

"Sure," she replies, blushing.

"Lunch?" I scream. The door shuts in my face.

*

That's the closest I've come to an actual prospective date with Zoe, so it leaves me on cloud nine. I skip past all my coworkers, exchanging pleasantries as I pass.

"Good morning, Betty. Don't you look beautiful today?"

"Well, oh my, looks like someone has a little pep in their step this morning!"

"Hello, everyone! Isn't today just a glorious day?"

"Well, looks like *someone* got laid last night," says Susie. Susie is a fiftieth-floor floozy who'll have sex with anyone, so long as they make a six-figure salary. She's also spread the clap around so liberally that she should get a standing ovation when she enters the building.

"Who's the lucky girl?" she asks, all flirty.

"Not you, sweets," I reply, brushing her cheek. Susie is always dressed to impress with short skirts and low-cut blouses. Strategic scarves cover her cleavage, depending on her mood, and she gets the attention of most. Not me, though. I tend to ignore those who scream for attention.

"I could make you feel that way too, you know," she insists.

"Well, my heart belongs to another, but how about you throw my boy Sid a bone?"

"Ew, gross!" she squeals. She isn't wrong; Sid isn't the most attractive guy. He's short, only standing about 5'6", overweight and never dresses to impress, wearing jeans and the same lime green polo shirt to work every day.

"Yeah, gross," exclaims Justin Beaver, her very metrosexual cubicle buddy. No prizes for guessing his nickname, although he does bear an amazing resemblance to the actual Justin Bieber.

"That guy is so gross and sweaty," he says, "and isn't he like a grade-B salary level?"

"Who the hell asked you, Beaver?" I reply, annoyed by his interjection.

"My name is pronounced 'Beäver'!" he growls.

"If my name sounded like a bratty teenage singer who needs to be bitch-slapped, I'd be pretty eager to clarify that, too."

"Screw you, Tyson!"

"Easy, Beaver, don't get your panties in a wad."

"Go screw yourself!" Justin replies, red-faced.

"I'll take a rain check," I shoot back. "As for you, Susie, stop dick-teasing Sid. He really likes you, and you know it. I see you messing with his mind."

She just laughs, as if to say she can do whatever she wants. What a bitch! I would never sleep with Susie, but poor Sid is madly in love with her, and she knows it. She ridicules him and makes him do crazy things for her, and he obeys her every command. We keep telling him she's crazy, but he doesn't want to hear about it. He just says one day he's going to prove us all wrong and sleep with her. There's a big office pool on it, but the smart money says it'll never happen.

I make my way into the server room, where I'll spend the rest of my day with my boys: Vegas, Fickle and Sid. The server room is the second most secure place in the building, just behind the seventy-fifth floor, and it's the IT safe haven. No one has access except us IT folk, which means no one can find us when we're in here. As you walk in, there's a comforting hum coming from the racks and racks of server fans. It helps to drown out the mundane chatter of the offices beyond. This is where we talk shit about everyone, tell Sid he's an idiot for trying to get in Susie's panties, watch Vegas update his office pools and where the guys have to listen to me talk about how I'm ever so close to my first date with the beautiful yet elusive woman from the seventy-fifth floor.

Swiping myself into the secure room, I only see Sid. He's quietly plugging away at a terminal located in one of the server racks.

"Where is everyone?" I yell.

"Vegas is out collecting money from his fat-asy draft," Sid replies, "and Fickle has been summoned to Grand's office."

"Man, poor Fickle, having to deal with Grand this early in the morning. One of these days he's gonna... Wait, did you say 'fat-asy' draft?"

"Yeah," Sid laughs. "It's Johnny's latest office pool. He started a wellness program where people can join to lose weight. He has weekly weigh-ins to track their progress and offer encouragement."

"That doesn't sound like something Vegas would get into, but hey, a noble cause."

"Well, not exactly," replies Sid. "Once he got the contestants all locked in, he started a secret fat-asy league where people can draft the participating chunk-butts for their team. Each week, players go head-to-head to see which team can lose the most weight. Remember last week when Paul slapped that donut out of Kathy's mouth and told her to get back on track? Well, she's on his fat-asy team."

"Holy shit, I do remember! I thought Paul was just being a dick, or suddenly cared for Kathy's health. Wow, Vegas is terrible, but also pretty damn brilliant!"

Sid nods and goes back to pounding at his keyboard.

"So, what are you doing over there?" I ask.

"Funny you should ask," he says as he matter-of-factly pounds the last few keys. "Come take a look."

As I look at the screen, I immediately see what Sid has achieved.

"You finally hacked into the security cameras!"

"Yep!" he responds proudly. Sid has spent a great deal of time trying to get full access to the building's security system.

"Did you get into—" I begin, but before I can finish, he cuts me off.

"No, still can't crack the seventy-fifth floor. They're using encryption that I've never seen before. It's like some NSA bullshit."

"It probably *is* the NSA," I reply. "You better stop trying to break into their system, or one day you may just disappear. You know, Jimmy-Hoffa style."

"Oh, don't worry about me; I'm spoofing Gerry Grand's IP address. All traffic ends up pointing right to him," he says, laughing.

Meanwhile, in Gerry Grand's office, Fickle is taking his daily sexual harassment.

"Hey, Fickle, get over here and tell me why my email isn't working."

Fickle walks over to take a look, only to see a video of a three-hundred-and-fifty-pound woman having hardcore sex with a three-foot midget.

"Jesus!" Fickle proclaims loudly. "I don't want to see this stuff, sir!"

Grand laughs and smacks Fickle on his ass.

"C'mon, now, don't tell me you're not into chubbies doing midgets! That's downright un-American!"

"Sir, what can I help you with, today?" Fickle asks with an almost sickened look on his face.

"Right, let's get to business. The first thing I need you to do is get my putter out of your ass!" Grand says as he picks up his putter and gooses the hell out of Fickle.

"C'mon, Mr. Grand! You're making me feel really uncomfortable."

"Hey, what's up your ass, besides my this?" Grand says laughing as he ram the end of his putter up Fick's ass. "You know, Jamison is leaving at the end of this month, and I've been eyeballing you for that promotion, but not if you're going to be a tight-ass prude!"

"Jamison is leaving?" Fickle says, suddenly intrigued.

"That's right. I'm naming his replacement this morning at the executive meeting, and you're on my shortlist. This is a tight network though, and I need someone I can trust; someone who can take the heat and has thick skin. Is that you, Fickle, or am I wasting my time with you?"

"Sir, I'm your man. I've been waiting my whole life for this opportunity. I won't let you down, sir."

Fickle has worked his whole life to move up the corporate ladder. He always dresses in expensive suits, looking presentable with his dark hair perfectly styled, his face clean-shaven and his smile sparkling with whitener. He's reached this moment through pure brown-nosing.

"We'll see! Now, come here and watch this midget drill the shit out of this behemoth. Man, how does he even get it in there?"

"Yes, sir," Fickle responds, as he reluctantly walks behind the desk to watch the video over Grand's shoulder.

"You don't have a chub, do you, Fickle?" Grand asks as he pokes the front of Fickle's pants with his putter.

"No sir, no chub here," Fickle says with a sigh.

Back in the server room, Johnny Vegas strolls in to find me and Sid voyeuristically checking out the security cameras. Vegas is a perfect Italian stereotype. He has slicked-back, jet black hair, with the most awesome mustache a man can grow. He looks like he's right out of the mob.

"Hi, Vegas, what's happening?" I say.

"Hey guys, how's it going?" he replies sulkily.

"What's wrong?" Sid asks.

"Just had a long meeting with the HR director. Turns out some of my office pools have garnered the attention of the employee ethics committee, so I was formally put on notice to shut them all down."

"Oh man, that sucks!" I reply. "Well, don't be too down. Look, Sid hacked into the security system, so we have a new pastime."

"Guys!" Sid exclaims excitedly. "Speaking of that, you're gonna want to take a look at this!"

We all peer into the monitor and notice military personnel walking into the building.

"My money says they're heading to the seventy-fifth," I say.

"That's a sucker's bet," says Vegas.

CHAPTER 3
THE GENESIS PROJECT

Z OOK STEPS OUT of his limo, a small entourage of ass-kissers and tourists surrounding him. Adjusting his cufflinks and tie, he rises, proceeding to the building's front entrance. Flanking him is Jeremy Jacobs, Zook's right-hand man. If Zook gives an order, it's usually Jacobs who does the dirty work. As they walk towards the building, you can see all the eyes falling on him. While onlookers idolize him and clamor for his autograph, employees fear him and work to get out of his line of sight. As he struts into the building, Jacobs clears the way to Zook's private elevator, pulling out a swipe card and opening the elevator doors just as Zook walks up to enter.

Jacobs steps in next to him and barks, "This is a private elevator. Take the public elevator."

The door closes and the elevator rises to top floor, the penthouse suite, which belongs solely to Zook.

"Today's an important day for Zook Enterprise," Zook says as he grooms himself in the reflection of the mirrored elevator.

"Yes, sir. Everything is in place, as you requested."

"Everything?" Zook asks.

"Yes, sir. Everything is precisely as you requested."

"Good! We need to make sure these idiots understand what needs to be done to eradicate radical Islamic terrorists. Extremism can only be met with extremism. When our weak-ass government realizes that, they'll be looking to me to fix it, and I'll give them Genesis! That's what the people want. To wipe these animals of the face of the earth. Our president can't even say radical Islamic extremism. Can you believe that? She's so weak! Well, I'm not weak! I'll not only say radical Islamic extremism, I will show my power and send them all straight to the gates of hell. If our government can't act, if they can't show strength, I won't hesitate to work with our overseas allies to sell Genesis to those in power who have the balls to protect this world from violent aggressors. We need these guys to start thinking like our founding fathers did and do what it takes to protect this great nation."

"The clients will be here at nine-thirty," says Jacobs. "They've been in contact to say how much they're looking forward to seeing how you solved the problem of containment."

"Containment! Since when do these folks care about the ripple effects of combat?" Zook says, agitated. "What I'm giving them is the perfect weapon, and they're worried about containment? That's what oceans are for!"

"Yes, sir," Jacobs agrees.

"I'll show them some containment strategies, but they better hope and pray they're satisfied with what I already have. I've invested way too much money for this deal to fall through on a formality."

"You make sure all goes well today, Jacobs!" cries Zook, as the elevator opens on a beautiful office suite with all the luxurious fittings of a billionaire. "If it looks like things are going south, I won't hesitate to initiate my plan B!"

"Yes, sir," Jacobs replies loyally. "I'll make sure today is a great day for Zook Enterprise, no matter which way the deal goes."

"Good. Leave me, for now. Come get me in thirty minutes."

"Yes, sir," Jacobs replies, slowly closing the double doors behind him.

Down in the lobby, men in dark suits, and a few in high-ranking military uniforms, are loitering with purpose. Along with the black SUVs outside, they aren't an unprecedented sight at Zook Towers. Military personnel are regular customers for Zook, and they're familiar with the building. Gathering together, they make their way to the elevator, and one of them pulls out a swipe card, entering the elevator and selecting the seventy-fifth floor.

No one says a word on the ride up, but once the door opens, they're greeted by Zoe.

"Good morning, gentlemen. Welcome to Zook Labs. May I ask that you all enter the presentation room down the hall on your right. Please leave your personal items here, including any weapons or communication devices. Mr. Zook and Dr. Flemming will be with you shortly."

The men all place their handguns and phones in bins and proceed down the hall. Zoe trails as they enter the presentation room.

"Make yourself comfortable, gentlemen. The presentation will begin shortly," she says, closing the door as she exits the room.

Sure enough, it's only minutes before Zook and Jacobs step off the personal elevator and onto the seventy-fifth floor.

Waiting their arrival is an older woman, with long gray hair wearing a lab coat. "Good morning, Mr. Zook," Dr. Flemming says, extending her hand. Dr. Flemming is the best; a world-renowned scientist and the lead for Zook's pet project. She took some heat in the industry for 'selling out' and leaving the public field for the private sector, but only the best for Mr. Zook. Still, her knowledge of biogenetics is second to none, and whatever her colleagues think of her personally, they respect her work.

"Showtime," Zook responds, his face grim, and Jacobs says nothing.

"Certainly," replies Dr. Flemming, "let's get right to it! The presentation is all set in the experimentation room."

Zook, Jacobs and Dr. Flemming head down the hall to their waiting guests.

"All needs to go perfectly, today," Zook tells Dr. Flemming.

"We'll do our best," she agrees, "but I'm simply not comfortable in regards to containment."

"Don't you worry about that; that's my job," Zook snaps. "You just make sure the biological agent works as intended."

"Yes, Mr. Zook," says Dr. Flemming, seemingly defeated. Zook throws open the presentation room door.

"Gentlemen, thank you for coming down! I won't waste your time here, so let's get right to business. Dr. Flemming, please show us the experimentation room."

Dr. Flemming nods and walks over to the bunker station, typing on the terminal keyboard. After a few clicks, a dividing wall separates, revealing an oversized and completely padded room. A thick layer of glass stands between the two rooms; Zook's staff and the military personnel on one side, and fifteen chimpanzees on the other.

"What you're about to see is the most effective combat neutralizer ever known. We call it Genesis. Behind the two-pane glass, you'll see the chimps are interacting normally. What they don't know is that one of their furry little friends has been injected with a biological serum. The serum will be released into its bloodstream according to a timing agent. Before that happens, can anyone identify our subject? Anyone?" The crowd all step forward to inspect the chimpanzees.

"Dr. Flemming," Zook says assertively. Flemming looks down at the timer, which is coming up on zero.

"Three," she says, sweat beading her brow, "two, one..."

As she reaches the end of her countdown, the crowd waiting eagerly, one of the chimpanzees drops straight to the ground. A couple of the chimps make their way over, while some start to frantically run around the room, as if somehow anticipating what's coming next.

A sense of calm falls over the chimps, a moment of silence and stillness broken by the downed chimp springing over the crowded simians. His eyes are gray and lifeless, his breathing deep. Without warning, he rumbles with a tremendous growl and swiftly rips into the neck of his closest companion. Now, the chimps are screaming frantically. Some try to get away, bouncing off the walls of the padded room, while others try to help their injured friend. It's too late, the victim is dead, and the attacker jumps, fangs bared, ripping into the head of the closest chimp. Blood is splattered all over the walls and glass.

As the watchers gasp and murmur, the slain chimp slowly comes to its feet. With familiar, lifeless eyes, it looks around amid the chaos, and then lunges teeth-first into the first chimp it can reach.

"Jesus, they're like zombies!" says one military onlooker. "It's like watching *The Walking Dead*!"

In less than three minutes, it's over. The previously sterile room is now blood-soaked, crowded with mindless chimpanzees. Without any life in the room, the chimps are docile, meandering around like a bloody, ape version of *One Flew Over the Cuckoo's Nest*.

"Christ," says a voice in the crowd, "I have never seen anything like that in my entire life, and I have seen a lot of shit in my life!"

"So, gentlemen," crows Zook, "you have now seen Genesis decimate and neutralize. In ninety seconds, this group of fifteen chimps, which were so vibrant and full of life, are now brainless, lifeless husks. We crunched the numbers, and our data shows that releasing this agent into a single person will eliminate a hundred-thousand-strong army in under forty-eight hours. All without putting a single American boot on the ground or life on the line."

A low murmur spreads across the room like wildfire. Some in the room are clearly impressed, whispering gleefully, while others are straight-faced. Some even seem nauseous from the bloodbath.

"What we have here, gentlemen," Zook continues, "is the ultimate weapon America needs to eradicate terror. A goal we've been craving since the creation of this great nation! Peace on Earth."

The room breaks out into applause, and Zook raises his hands in the air, bathing in the monumental moment. As the applause dies down, one man in a black suit steps forward.

"What about containment?" he asks.

"I didn't catch your name," Zook replies.

"That's because I didn't give it. Some of us in this room are well aware of this bio-agent's capabilities. What we want to know is what you've done to improve containment."

"Well," Zook says confidentially, "for that, I'll turn you over to Dr. Flemming. Dr. Flemming, please indulge our guest and explain the improvements we've made with containment."

The group turn their attention to Dr. Flemming, who is still staring at the window through which she just witnessed devastating carnage.

"Dr. Flemming!" Zook repeats impatiently.

"Yes?" she asks, snapping out of her trance.

"This gentleman was asking about containment. Can you let him know what improvements we've made?"

"Yes, of course. We have improved both effectiveness and containment by adding an agent that rapidly accelerates the carrier's metabolism. What you witnessed here is an example: they were so ravenous that they instinctively attacked. It's similar to a fish attacking a lure; no matter how full the fish is, it has an instinctive need to attack. Hence its effectiveness and reliability. When you take a living thing with a metabolism this accelerated and deprive it of a food source, you put a timer on its survival. Now that these chimpanzees have no way to replenish themselves, they will expire over the next twelve to twenty-four hours."

"So the answer is to let them go hungry?" asked the black-suited man.

"Precisely!. That's the theory."

"How long would this depletion process take with a human?"

"Well, a lot depends on size, of course, and a few other secondary factors, and we of course haven't tested it on an actual human but I would say probably no longer than two to three days."

"Well, there's also napalm," Zook adds, laughing. Having regained the room's attention, he presses a button on the keyboard that sets the entire padded room into a fiery blaze. The chimps blood soaked bodies are now in flames as they continue to roam. One chimp senses life in the other room and throws himself against the window with the gaze of gray death peering through the eyes of the onlookers. As his scorched fur gives way to burnt flesh it becomes too much for some and they look away in disgust. Slowly, one by one, each chimp falls and becomes a completely motionless ball of fire. Apart from the crackling flames, the room is once again silent.

"So, gentlemen, any questions?" Zook asks as the wall folds back, hiding the smoldering massacre.

"I don't have a question," says the man in black, "but I do have a statement. What you have created here has not only compromised national security, but the very safety of humanity on this earth. This is no weapon to promote peace; it's a weapon that threatens peace every bit as much as it does existence."

"Now wait a second!" Zook spits back. "What we've created here evens the playing field against religious radicals! When you're dealing with the type of extreme terrorism America deals with on a daily basis, with those who threaten a holy war, you can't intimidate them with bombs, guns, chemical agents or tough talk. They're not afraid of dying and they're not afraid of *you*. They're fighting for their god! What you have to do is bring the wrath of God, of biblical, apocalyptic proportions, to their front doorstep! It's only when they see the workings of God's fury that they'll fall to their knees and beg forgiveness. *Gentlemen*, I am giving you Genesis! It's our new beginning."

The room is silent for a few moments while Zook's monologue is digested.

"In the name of national security, and in accordance with the National Defense Act," drawls the man in black, "we are temporarily detaining all personnel on this floor and confiscating any and all bio-agents."

"This is outrageous! I'm a patriot! I'm calling my lawyer!"

"Officers, please escort Mr. Zook to his office, where he can call his lawyer."

As two MPs walk towards Mr. Zook, the billionaire shares a look with Jacobs.

"Dr. Flemming," continues the man in black, "and the rest of you, you may go back to your offices, to the employee lounge or you may stay here, but please, no one is to attempt to leave the building until told otherwise. If everyone cooperates, this will all be over shortly. Thank you for your cooperation."

As Dr. Flemming walks down the hall to her office, she's followed by Jacobs. He quickly catches up, grabs her by her arm and hisses, "I need you to escort me to the lab!"

"You're not authorized to go into the lab, Jacobs. You know that."

"I'm not going to ask again!" he growls, drawing her eyes down to the silenced pistol he's aiming at her side. "You panic or say a word, I will kill you where you stand. You understand?" She nods in acknowledgement, and they hastily make their way to the lab. As Dr. Flemming swipes them in with her security card, Jacobs is already moving forward.

"Now, take me to Genesis!"

CHAPTER 4
THE BREACH

FICKLE WALKS INTO the server room and sees us all hovering around the terminal.

"Hey fellas, what's up?"

"Yo Fickle, how's it going? How was Gerry?" I reply.

"Same as always. He made me watch thirty minutes of midget porn and now I want to vomit, but other than that, I'm doing pretty damn good!"

"Really, what gives?"

Fickle is one of my best buds, but he usually spends his time in a constant 'Debbie Downer' state. He hates Gerry Grand, his job, his apartment, his car, his clothes, his life, everything.

"Well," he says now, with a grin, "you're looking at the new chief technology officer of IT operations."

"No shit!" I say excitedly.

"Awesome, Fick!" Vegas laughs. "You're going to be a total asshole now. I'm going to start calling you 'Fick the Dick'."

"So proud of you, Fick," adds Sid. "You've put up with Grand enough; I'm glad to see it paid off, although I guess you don't want to see what we're doing over here, now."

Fickle walks up to the terminal to peer over Sid's shoulder.

"Holy shit," he says, "is that what I think it is?"

"Yep, finally hacked into the building's security cameras."

"Damn, man! Well, I'm not CTO yet, so I can enjoy this for a little while longer. Hey, can you access the executive conference room camera?"

"Sure can," Sid responds. It takes him just a few minutes to comb over the hundreds of cameras before he locks in on the seventieth-floor executive conference room. He quickly isolates the camera feed so it's the only video showing on the terminal.

"Here it is," he says excitedly. The video clearly shows Gerry Grand and four other men sitting at the conference table.

"That's awesome!" says Fickle. "I bet they're talking about the CTO position right now. Is there sound?"

"There is, but we don't have speakers hooked up here."

"Will these work?" I ask, pulling a set of earbuds from my front pocket.

"Yep, bring them here," Sid exclaims. I grab one earbud while Fickle grabs the other, and we wait anxiously for Sid to plug in the other end. Suddenly, there's talking.

"Holy shit!" Fickle cries. "I can hear them!"

As we listen in, Gerry Grand says, "Okay, gentlemen, we need to discuss Jamison's departure."

"Here it is!" cheers Fickle.

"After looking over all the internal applicants, I've decided to give the promotion to Kyle Thompson. He was the only real prospect for this job, and we think he'll fit right in with the team. Thompson, get in here!"

Kyle Thompson walks into the room and everyone stands up, clapping. I slowly look up to see Fickle's face. He stands there, holding the earbud in his left ear, completely emotionless for a good thirty seconds.

"Fick, buddy... I'm so sorry, man."

"What happened?" Sid demands. "Fick, you look like someone just murdered a puppy. Will someone talk to me?"

Fickle drops the earbud, taking a step back as he wipes his eyes.

"That's okay, the job went to Kyle Thompson. Good for him. Kyle's a good guy and a hard worker."

"I'm really sorry, Fick," Vegas says.

"You didn't want to work for that dick, anyways!" I cry out. "The guy's a prick, and you deserve better!"

"No, it's all good, fellas," Fick responds, regaining his composure. "I'm fine with it, I really am."

We all know he's not fine with it, but what can you say to a guy who just had his dream job ripped from under him? There's a short silence as we all search for the right thing to say, when suddenly Sid's phone goes off. His ringtone is the chorus to Marvin Gaye's *Sexual Healing*, which he set up for when Susie calls.

"I have to get this, guys!" Sid yells excitedly. "This is Sid, how can I help you?"

"Sid! Whatever it is, don't do it!" I scream as he walks out of the server room. I frantically refocus on the terminal to take control of the cameras.

"What's up, Tyson?" Vegas asks, nonplussed.

"I'm pretty sure that was Susie. She won't stop screwing with his mind. Ten bucks says he's heading over to her desk."

"I will take that bet," says Vegas, reaching into his pocket to pull out some cash. I quickly scan through the dozens of video feeds and lock in on the suite where Susie sits. Sure enough, Sid walks up to her.

"Pay up, Vegas!"

"Can't believe I took that bet," Vegas seethes, dropping a ten spot into my hand.

"Hey Susie, what's up?" Sid asks excitedly.

"Hey there, Siddie-Poo! I left my card at home today and don't have any money for lunch. Can you loan me thirty dollars?"

"Well, how about we go out for lunch, my treat?"

"Oh, so sorry, sweetie; I already have lunch plans with Justin," she pouts.

"I guess I could loan you some money," he says, pulling out his wallet, "but I think this makes, like, six hundred dollars you owe me."

"Don't be silly," Susie giggles. "I'll pay you back."

"No, seriously, I'm pretty sure you owe me like six hundred bucks, or something close. I have a running tally going at my desk."

"I'll tell you what," she whispers, leaning in close. "How about you meet me in the storage closet in ten minutes and I'll pay off that debt?"

"For real?" Sid asks, barely able to contain his excitement.

"Yes, for real. Now, go get ready before I change my mind."

There's nothing else to clarify; rumor is pretty clear about exactly which storage closet Susie uses for her hookups.

"Now, where *is* he going?" Vegas asks, watching from the security camera as Sid skips away from Susie's desk.

"Double or nothing he's going to get her a cup of coffee," I say confidently.

"Deal!" Vegas exclaims.

"Man, you really do have a gambling problem. Hey, Fick! You want to get some of this action?" I shout over to Fick, who's sitting at a small desk in the corner of the server room. He looks up and tries to seem interested, but quickly bows his head back down to his sulking state.

"Man, we really need to get Fick out of his mood," I say to Vegas.

"*Ha!*" Vegas bellows, not even hearing me. "He's going to the storage closet!"

I look down at the video feed to see Sid open the supply closet door, look around stealthily and then close the door behind him. "Looks like we're even, Tyson. Give me my ten back!"

"No way is she going to meet him in there. Should we go get him?" I ask Vegas.

"Nah, he needs some tough love, man. Maybe he'll learn that she's nothing but a gold digger."

"'Gold Digger'? Who are you, Kayne West? You gonna interrupt my Grammy speech, next?"

"You know what I mean. He needs to see just how much of a bitch she really is."

"Agreed. Tough love it is."

"Jacobs, you know I can't do that!" Dr. Flemming cries out.

"Don't make me ask you again, Doctor!" Jacobs snarls, pushing the pistol into her temple. "Your life depends on it."

Breathing heavily, fearing for her life, Dr. Flemming walks reluctantly over to a glass room. She pauses before the various equipment that will accept her ID and numeric code.

"Please," she begs, "you don't have to do this!"

"All I'm doing is protecting your hard work, Doctor. These guys are coming in here to steal it. I'm looking out for your, and the company's, best interests. Now, stop stalling and open the door!"

Dr. Flemming proceeds to punch in her code, and they both step into the chilled, glass room.

"Those are the bio-agents, over there," Dr. Flemming says, pointing to a small, locked medical case.

"Well, open it up!"

She pulls out her keys and fiddles with them, trying to find the right one. Finding it, she takes a deep breath, then inserts the key and turns it gently. As the door opens, Jacobs reaches high in the air, extending his arm to full length, then swiftly thrusts down with the butt of his gun, cracking the back of Dr. Flemming's skull.

"Thank you so much, Doctor!" Jacobs says, kneeling down over her unconscious body. Getting back to his feet, he looks through the open cabinet, quickly spotting what he's looking for: T1Z4 agents.

"Hello, Genesis!" he exclaims. He extracts twenty vials and places them in a small, plastic canister, then scans the room for his next objective. Finding a hypodermic needle, he makes his way back to Dr. Flemming. He reaches into the plastic canister and pulls out a single vial of the agent, then bends down to whisper in Dr. Flemming's ear.

"Congratulations, Doctor. You're patient zero. It all starts with you."

He flips the bottle over and slides the needle into the vial, drawing in the agent. After he reaches forty CCs of the dark, mahogany liquid, he pulls out the syringe, gently sweeps Dr. Flemming's hair out the way and plunges it into her neck.

"Happy hunting!" he chuckles as he stands back up, hiding his gun within his suit jacket. Mission accomplished, he grabs his canister and charges towards the exit.

As he walks out into the hallway he screams, "Help! Someone, *help!* Something is wrong with Dr. Flemming!"

"What happened?" asks a member of military personnel, his colleagues streaming into the lab.

"I don't know! I walked in and saw her on the ground. Someone, please, go help her!"

As the men rush by, Jacobs' frantic concern drains away. Straight-faced, he makes his way to Zook's private elevator and enters, canister in hand. Zoe, hearing the commotion, comes around the corner and sees Jacobs standing in the elevator.

"Jacobs, what's going on?" she asks as she looks down, noticing the canister tucked under his arm. He simply stares straight ahead, as if he was looking straight through her. Zoe takes a step towards the elevator as it starts to close. It's only in the moment before the door closes that Jacobs reacts. He looks directly at her and smiles.

There's a slight tap on the door of the storage closet, and a very anxious and very naked Sid responds, "Come on in." Suddenly, the door rips open, revealing more than a dozen people. They're laughing, pointing and snapping pictures on their smartphones. Sid scans the room frantically, looking for some kind of cover. He reaches for the first thing he sees, which is a mop soaking in a bucket of filthy water. It's enough to cover himself, but now he has filthy water cascading down his thighs. In the midst of the crowd of onlookers, he sees Susie laughing and pointing along with everyone else.

"Susie? How could you do this to me?"

"Did you really think I was going to go in there and screw your brains out?" she laughs. "Not while I'm alive and breathing!"

"But I love you," Sid responds, completely dumbfounded by her betrayal.

"Ew, you're so gross! Please, someone shut the door before I vomit."

"See you, lover boy!" laughs Justin Beaver, slamming the storage room door in Sid's face. As the belly laughs fade away, he drops the mop and slowly starts to cry.

There are several men kneeling around the doctor.

"Is she okay?" one bystander asks. "It looks like she hit her head."

"Gentlemen!" Zoe shouts, running into the lab. "This is a highly restricted area. You need to get out of here, now!"

"The doctor is hurt!"

Suddenly, the doctor's breathing gets shallower and more frantic.

"Is she hyperventilating?"

"Doctor, are you okay?"

Her eyes flicker open, almost opaque.

"Jesus!" says one of the men. Without warning, Dr. Flemming lunges, her wide-open mouth closing on the neck of a concerned helper.

"Oh *God!* Someone, help me!"

Before anyone can move, Dr. Flemming is onto her next victim, digging her teeth into the side of his face. As the rest of the men back up, her first victim climbs to his feet with the same opaque eyes.

"Oh shit!" Zoe screams, turning to run out of the room. She reaches behind her jacket and pulls out a radio. "Attention, we have a code one! I repeat, a code one! Prepare a lockdown of seventy-five, this is not a drill!"

She makes her way down the hall, looking back to see three men, seemingly ravenous, chasing after her. Knowing she's not going to outrun them, she drops her radio, reaches back and pulls out a semi-automatic handgun. She starts firing, hitting the first two in their chests, but it does little to dissuade them. Refocusing her aim, she shoots one of them in the head, stopping him dead in his tracks. Two more shots and all three are lying motionless in the hallway. She reaches for her radio, but five infected men charge out of the lab, tailed by Dr. Flemming. Zoe turns and runs, heading for the lockdown doors.

"I said code one!" she shouts into the radio, seeing that they aren't closing. "Jimmy, close the doors!"

There's no answer. She hesitates for a second; she only has a limited opportunity to get outside the containment doors, but it won't matter if the floor isn't sealed. Instead of running for safety, she heads for the control room, quickly swiping herself in and shutting the door behind her. The room is empty, but she can hear the infected scratching to get in. She darts to the control terminal, where she can see all the video feeds on the seventy-fifth floor. On every feed, people are being attacked and devoured. She sees Jimmy, lifeless on the ground, only recognizable by his security guard outfit, while two of the infected feed on his remains.

The elevator door opens on Zook's suite, where he sits at his desk. Jacobs steps out, past the MPs guarding the elevator.

"You guys need to get down there and help!" he barks. "Something awful has happened, and they need all the firepower they can get."

"We have our orders" says one of the MPs.

"Just call down there and see," Jacobs orders. The other MP walks to Zook, who is already dialing the phone.

"Is everything okay down there?" asks the MP, taking the headset. Distant screams are his only answer.

"Come on, let's go!" he says.

"What about Zook?"

"He's not going anywhere, are you, Zook?"

"Where am I going to go?" Zook replies. The MPs run to the elevator and head down while Zook looks over to Jacobs.

"We good?"

"Yes, sir, we are good."

"Excellent! What we are doing today will go down in history as the day I saved America and made it like it used to be. Come on. Our chariot awaits," says Zook, leading the way to the helicopter pad just outside the penthouse suite.

Zoe frantically initiates the lockdown of the seventy-fifth floor. As the steel bay doors close, she keeps her eyes on the escape routes. She sees the two MPs step off Zook's elevator only to be instantly swarmed by the infected. The doors aren't quick enough, and she watches as a crowd of infected make their way through before they seal.

"No!" she shrieks. She takes a deep breath, picks up the phone and dials a number. "We have a breach from the seventy-fifth."

"How bad?" asks security control.

"Bad! Please commence immediate lockdown of both towers."

"Roger that."

"We're on a code red lockdown, gentlemen," shouts the controller, down on the first floor. "Seal the doors!"

The terminal operators glance at each other for a moment, then start typing. Alarms sound in the building, and emergency lights flash as onlookers look around in amazement. Then, solid steel doors drop from the walls, covering each and every possible exit. Once the doors are down, the alarm stops.

"The building is completely contained, sir."

"It's in God's hands now. If you're a god fearing person you better start praying."

CHAPTER 5
LOCKDOWN

IN THE SERVER room, we're now in our typical mid-morning state of relaxation. I'm half-asleep with a bag of Doritos in my lap, Vegas is playing Texas hold 'em on one of the desk computers and Fick is balled up in a chair, slowly rocking and chewing his fingernails. Suddenly, the regular lights go out, the emergency lights come on and an alarm starts to sound.

"That's new," Vegas says, looking up.

"What the hell?" I yell, as we all jump up, trying to figure out what's going on. The alarm is so blaring that I can barely focus on why it's going off.

"Maybe it's a test?" Fickle yells, but I can barely hear him through the deafening sound. It doesn't sound like a test; it sounds like the type of alarm you hear when a nuclear power plant starts to melt down. All I'm waiting for is a computerized voice to come over the PA, letting me know the building will self-destruct in three minutes.

"I don't have a good feeling about this," Vegas blurts out, panicking. "Let's get out of here."

We walk to the server room doors and push down on the handle, but the door doesn't open.

"What the hell, man! We're locked in!" Vegas shouts, now in full panic mode.

"I think it's the power!" says Fick. "I'm guessing the power outage won't let the door open."

"What kind of door locks when there's no power!" cries Vegas, pushing desperately at the door. "It's a damn *door!* How sophisticated does it have to be?"

"Hey, man, we're in the data-center," I reply. "This is one of the areas they need to be secure. It's probably just a security feature. It's all fine; the doors will open soon, let's not lose our shit!"

"Where the hell is Sid?" Vegas replies, practically hyperventilating. "*He* could get these doors open!"

Sid, now dressed, is sitting on the floor of the maintenance closet. He hears the alarms going off, but he doesn't seem to care about the warning.

"I hope a plane flies into the side of this building and kills us *all!* Stupid Susie and her stupid face with her stupid friends. I'm not leaving! I'm staying in this closet forever!"

*

About Sid

Sid is a great guy, and one of the most loyal friends I've ever had. He also happens to be quite brilliant. I met him when I started here a few years ago, and once I got past the tics, weirdness and social mishaps, I got to see the real Sid. He has social limitations, which makes it difficult for him to fit in, and especially to understand when he's not fitting in. That's why Susie pisses me off so much. Bottom line, she knows he isn't like everyone else, and she exploits that and continues to mess with him. She's pure evil and deserving of every single STD she ever gets.

*

As people on all floors try to make sense of the alarms, some slowly make their way to the stairwells, some try for the elevator and some simply refuse to move, thinking it's just another false alarm. As the staircases start to get jammed, packed with one hundred floors of people making their way downstairs, the commotion from the higher floors begins to grow louder.

"Listen, everyone!" screams an authoritative voice from the fiftieth floor, his voice echoing up and down the stairwell. He removes his jacket slowly and loosens his tie. "We need to slowly make our way downstairs in an orderly fashion. Please, head down to the lobby. Thank you."

"What's going on up there?" asks an older business man, squinting up at the faint sounds of screaming.

"I'm not sure," says an associate. "It's probably just people panicking."

As the screaming and commotion get closer, an African American woman peeks up through the center of the staircase in an attempt to see what's going on.

"What the..." she murmurs, trying to focus on a strange shape that's falling towards her. She steps back just in time, avoiding the body that spins past.

"What the hell was that?" the older gentleman screams. The crowd in the stairwell stare at each, unable to believe what they've seen, but not for long, as it's only moments until another body slams into the railing. The impact splits the head, and it explodes in blood and brain, the railing ringing like a gong. There's another brief moment of silence, the group coated in human tissue and membrane, brains dripping from their business suits and noses.

As an office worker wearing a plaid business suit slowly wipes the sludge from his brow and shows his hand to the others in the stairwell, he exclaims, "Let's get the hell out of here!"

Panic ensues, and the assembled staff start trampling their way down the overcrowded stairs. People are pushing and stepping over each other, a frantic herd making its way to the lobby, unable to outrun the screams from the floors above.

"Go, go, go!" yells a middle-aged woman in a power suit, trying to push her way through the packed crowd. "They're coming!"

"Who's coming?" cries another woman, pulling up her pant leg to reach down and unstrap her high heels for better mobility.

"*Help!*" Vegas screams as he bangs on the server room door, taking a moment to look through the peephole to see if anyone can hear him.

"Vegas, calm down! There's no use in screaming and acting like a lunatic. Everyone left. Let's look for something to pry the door open."

There's a knock on the door.

"Hello?" Vegas screams.

"Johnny, is that you? It's Betty. What are you doing in there? Don't you know everyone is evacuating?"

"Oh my God, thank you, God! Betty, God bless you! Yes, it's me. I'm in here with Fickle and Tyson; we're locked in the room."

"Well, you boys just hang in there. I'm going to get some help!"

"Thank you so much, Betty! You're the best!"

"Okay, boys. I'll be back in a jiffy!"

Vegas looks through the peephole and sees Betty turn to walk away. As she does so, a man staggers towards her.

"Who is that?" Vegas murmurs, refocusing for a better look. As things swim into focus, the man lunges at Betty, sinking his teeth into the side of her face. He hits a vein, and blood spurts three feet into the air.

"*No!*" Vegas shouts, banging on the door. "What the…"

"What the hell is going on out there?" I scream as Fickle and I run over.

"Some guy is *biting* Betty on her face! *Hey!* Get the hell off of her!" Vegas screams, slapping the door, his eye fixed on the peephole.

"Let me see!" I shout, pushing Vegas aside.

"What's going on?" Fickle exclaims. I put my eye to the peephole hesitantly, not really wanting to see what's going on, but needing to validate Johnny's behavior. As my eye focuses, I see Betty's lifeless body on the ground. A strange figure is stooped over her, gnawing on her face.

"What the hell is going on?"

"I don't know, man," Vegas replies, his voice shaking. "Is Betty okay? Is that guy still there? Is she dead?"

As he speaks, the 'guy' stops and whips his head in the direction of the door.

"Holy shit!" I cry. "That's Justin!"

"Who's Justin? *Justin* is the guy eating Betty's face? Is he on bath salts or something?"

"Shh! He's looking this way."

As Justin gets to his feet, Betty's body starts to move.

"Betty's alive! She's getting up! Betty, run! *Run!*"

Hearing us, Justin hurls himself at the server room door.

"Jesus! Justin is trying to get in here, now! He has to be on drugs or something."

Betty is up now and, like Justin, she turns towards the door.

"What's happening now?" Fickle asks nervously.

"Damn, Betty is missing half her face! Why isn't she running?"

In fact, she is, and she hits the server room door with incredible impact. I jump back, startled.

"Whoa! Betty's trying to get in here, now. She's acting just as whack as Justin!"

"What the hell is going on?" Vegas says as we all step back from the door.

"Shit, man, I hate to say it…" I reply.

"Say what?" Fickle asks.

"Everyone needs to find a weapon," I answer. "Find what you can, fast!"

"Tyson!" Vegas screams. "What is *going on* out there?"

I take a slow, deep breath, knowing Fickle and Vegas are now completely focused on every word coming out of my mouth. I know that if I say what I'm thinking, it'll put them both in hysterics, but I can't stop myself.

"*Zombies!*"

In the stairwell, a secretary is focusing on the commotion from the floors above. She can hear the frantic footsteps coming ever closer and turns, hoping to dodge around what she thinks will be a herd of panicked office workers. As the crowd's shadow makes its way around the corner, her eyes fill with fear.

"What the fu—"

A woman in a power suit leaps down an entire flight of stairs, her incisors closing on the secretary's neck. As she sinks her teeth in, blood fountains out, coating the walls of the stairwell. Now laying over the fallen secretary like a stray dog grinding its teeth on a carcass, she looks up to see the panicked crowd of people stuck in the stairwell. She lets out a tremendous growl and, before anyone can react, a huge pack of infected round the corner and launch themselves into their stranded prey.

Down in the lobby, people are walking around calmly, completely unaware of the madness bearing down on them. All of a sudden, the doors to the stairwell fling wide open, violently banging into the wall as people push and scream their way out, sprinting over to the exit doors of tower one.

"No, no, *no!*" screams a balding businessman, realizing they're sealed. "We've got to get out of here!"

There's a sudden hush in the immense lobby as hundreds of people focus on the stairwell, and a rush of sprinting, infected zombies flood out, tearing a swathe through the lobby. Complete lunacy takes hold and, in the distance, the elevator doors open, spilling even more zombies into the lobby. The huge space pulses with the infected, scurrying quickly and efficiently between victims, devouring everything in their path. In mere minutes, the workers are completely overwhelmed by the flesh-hungry pack in a bloodbath of human carnage.

The lobby security personnel look on in complete horror. From the safety of their locked-down suite, they witness sheer terror from the multitude of security cameras. Their heads swivel from one screen to another as they try to make sense of it all.

"We have to help them!" one of the guards hollers desperately.

"Are you insane?" barks Derek, the lead security officer. "Take a good look at those cameras! We go out there and we're lunch at best. At worst, we turn into one of them! The only thing we can do is call it in and pray." He points to the other security guard. "Dylan, call it in!"

The remaining guard, Frank, focuses on the hundred different views he has of the building, each marred by a brutal attack. He focuses back on the lobby camera, which is a wide-angle view of the entire area.

"Dylan's calling it in," he murmurs, watching as thousands of people flee for their lives. "I guess I'll just pray."

Up in the security office on the seventy-fifth floor, Zoe is covering her mouth in shock as she takes in what she's seeing on her own screen.

"How did this happen?" she blurts out, already trying to

piece together some kind of timeline for the events that have brought her here. "Jacobs... Did he do this on purpose? Maybe the meeting didn't go as planned, and this was their way to hush things up."

Her mind is racing a million miles a minute, but the video feeds quickly win back her attention. Understanding that this is her new reality, she bursts into tears and covers her face completely.

CHAPTER 6
THE STORM BEFORE THE CALM

THE OUTSIDE OF Zook Towers is buzzing with activity. Fire trucks, police cars, SWAT tanks and crime scene tape keep onlookers and reporters outside the building's perimeter, while news helicopters circle above. A black sedan pulls up, and out steps a tall man. His hair is graying, and he's dressed in full police regalia, with all the medals and stripes of a high-ranking official.

"Can someone tell me what's going on, here?" he says impatiently.

"Good afternoon, Chief!" replies Captain Jeffords of the NYPD. "At approximately ten forty-five this morning, dispatch started receiving hundreds of calls reporting a terrorist attack on Zook Towers. The first batch of calls was due to an alarm going off in the building—"

"Captain, you're telling me this circus is all because of an alarm?"

"No, sir! Those were the first calls. Shortly after that, dispatch started receiving calls about terrorists physically attacking and killing people in the building."

"How many terrorists, and what kind of weaponry are we talking about?"

"Sir, we've been unable to ascertain how many, so far. The towers are completely sealed from the inside, and no groups have attempted to make contact or claim responsibility, at this time."

"Okay, but there are windows! Can we see what the hell's going on inside, Captain? We need to know exactly what we're dealing with and how much firepower these guys have!"

"Yes, sir!" says the captain. "We were able to obtain some video footage of the attacks from the floors above. The problem is, sir, the weapons they appear to be using."

"Come on, Captain, don't pussyfoot. What do they have?"

"It's their mouths, sir! They're attacking people with their mouths."

"What the hell do you mean, 'their mouths'?"

"Johnson," the captain cries, summoning over a SWAT officer, "show the chief the footage."

The chief leans in intently as the black screen of the officer's tablet fades away and the video starts to play. It's been taken from the perspective of the police helicopter, about sixty-five stories up. The chief's eyes widen as people frantically scramble for their lives, pursued by ravenous terrorists. A woman runs towards the window, throwing herself against it, trying to jump to her death to escape. As she meets the resistance of the fortified high-rise window, she makes eye contact with the helicopter hovering directly across from her. He sees the woman mouth 'Help me!' before a young man in a business suit slams into her from behind. After only a second or two of resistance, she submits to her captor and slowly slides down the window, leaving only a trail of blood.

The chief turns his back to the video and his officers, struggling to comprehend what he has just witnessed. With over thirty-five years of police experience in one of the most violent cities in America, he thought he'd seen it all. But this? This is too much to digest.

"Chief?" says Captain Jeffords. "We've fortified the perimeter and the building has pretty much locked itself down. We're trying to get those news helicopters out of here, but we're pretty sure they've already got the same kind of footage. Uh, Chief?"

"Okay," the chief replies tersely, turning back to his men. "It's only a matter of time before this becomes a full-on media nightmare. Let's get those helicopters grounded and everyone on-board searched and detained. One leak of flesh-eating terrorists will unleash hysterical panic of apocalyptic proportions, and we can't deal with that right now. Jesus, face-eating zombies in New York. I expect this shit in Florida, but New York?"

"You heard the chief," screams Captain Jeffords, "let's get those news choppers grounded, now!"

"Get a hold of Homeland Security, the National Guard and the FBI. Don't undersell it. We need the cavalry on this one."

"You got it, Chief!"

"You think the doors will hold?" Fickle asks.

"Be prepared for anything!" I yell, as the banging grows louder. We've equipped ourselves with makeshift weapons. Mine is, by far, the best; an old-school, industrial-strength paper cutter. The lever makes a perfect, albeit crude, machete. Vegas has taken the leg off a desk, but he's left one of the screws hanging out, which should do quite nicely for piercing skulls. Fick, on the other hand, has chosen a short-nosed number two screwdriver. We pleaded with him to get something more substantial, but he won't hear it. To be honest, I'm not sure me and the guys are capable of killing anyone. We're computer analysts, for heaven's sake. Our zombie expertise consist of *Call of Duty* in the evenings and Monday morning debriefings on the latest *The Walking Dead* episode. I don't think any of us are actually capable of 'nutting up', as Tallahassee from *Zombieland* suggests. I guess we're about to find out, because it's only a matter of time until the doors give way, then we'll see what we're capable of. As we anxiously wait for Betty and Justin to break down the doors, the lights come back on.

"The power's back," Vegas whispers. "What do you think that means?"

"Well, it means we can get out of the server room now," I laugh, and as if on cue, the banging stops. "After you, Vegas."

"Are... are they gone?" Fickle whimpers.

"I don't know," I say, my heart pounding a thousand beats a second. "Let me check the peephole."

I fix my eyes on the peephole. I see Betty and Justin, but they're facing away from us, over at a figure on the other side of the suite.

"It's Sid," I whisper. "Sid's alive!"

Fickle, Vegas and I share a quick moment of glee, before realizing that Sid is out there with two people who want to rip his face off. Worse, he may not even know it. There's a roar, and suddenly Betty and Justin are heading for Sid.

"No!" I scream, throwing the door open and sprinting towards Sid. Halfway there, I realize Vegas and Fickle have followed on instinct.

"Sid, run!" I yell as the infected close in on him. Sid doesn't hesitate, immediately turning and running down the hall. Not the most athletically gifted, I know he doesn't have a chance of outrunning anyone.

"Hey, Justin, come get some of this fresh blood!" I scream, as I pick up the closest thing I can find. I throw it, hitting Justin in the back of the head with a swingline stapler. Both Betty and Justin stop dead in their tracks and swing to face me.

"Oh, shit! *Run!*" I scream, forgetting that I'm a badass. Justin starts after me and I start to zigzag between desks, rolling chairs and whipping pens at him. I glance over to see Betty leaning over Vegas, trying to take a bite out of his throat, with Fickle trying to pull her away. After a few speedy evading maneuvers, I remember I have a badass machete in my hand. Why am I throwing pens at this thing? I do a quick circle around a desk, and as Justin comes around the other side, I take a full swing at the side of his head with my glorified cleaver. The machete sinks into the side of his skull, and it explodes, blood gushing from the open wound. Soaked in viscera, I pull back for another shot, and Justin tumbles backwards. I slash down once, and then again, but he remains prone on the floor. I know I'm panicking, but I'm also instinctual enough to make sure whatever Justin has turned into is no longer a threat. I try to absorb the horror of what I've just done, but as soon as I calm down a little, I realize Vegas and Fickle need my help. Betty seems to be an inch away from digging into Vegas' neck; I can hear her teeth chattering in anticipation. Fickle is on top of her, doing his best to get her off, but it's not working. She's voracious, focused on the pulsating heartbeat pounding through Johnny's neck. As I make my way over, Fickle reluctantly reaches into his pocket and pulls out his screwdriver, then jams it into the back of Betty's skull. He screams as he thrusts it in, and it makes it all the way through, exiting out of Betty's left eye socket and summoning a geyser of blood as she falls motionless on top of Vegas.

"Get her off of me!" Vegas screams, pushing and kicking her away. Fickle is staring at his hands, caught up in utter remorseful disgust. I reach them as Vegas manages to stand, hopping away from his attacker.

"Are you guys okay?"

"Yeah, I'm cool," Vegas replies, catching his breath. "Dude, you're covered in blood! You look ridiculous."

"*Me?* Look at *you*, man!" I laugh, hysterical. "You have blood and… and eye goo all over your face."

Really, I'm barely keeping it together. Of course this isn't funny, it's tragic; Betty was the nicest lady, and we're standing over her bloody body. Part of me wants to mourn her, and Justin too, but another part knows that there'll be a lot more of this before we get out of the building. I push my emotions down; they won't help me now, and I need to keep everyone else stable, even aggressive. It might be callous, but humor is our best way of coping with what's ahead.

"Man," says Vegas, awed, "Justin's head popped like a watermelon that was being smashed by Gallagher! It was freaking intense. Oh, and I hit him with a stapler! I always wanted to whip a stapler at someone. That felt great!"

I'm glad to see he's thinking along the same lines.

"What's wrong with you two?" Fickle screams through tears. "We just killed two people; our coworkers, our friends, and you guys are making jokes?"

"Screw you, Fick!" I scream. I hear my voice break, I know I'm unstable, but with everything else I'm repressing, I just have to go with it. "I killed *Justin*. Justin wasn't my friend; he was an fake asshole. He said stupid bullshit like, 'Looks like someone has a case of the Mondays' and '*Hump day*, whoop, whoop!' I did the world a favor killing his stupid ass! *You*, however, you killed Betty! Betty was a sweetheart. She made us coffee and always told us how wonderful we were! She was a saint, and you stabbed her in the back of the neck with a screwdriver like an assassin! Screw you for trying to make me feel bad!"

"Hey, guys, let's keep it together," Vegas says calmly, slipping between me and Fickle. "We can't turn on each other. We need to keep our wits about us and work together."

"You're right," I say. My emotions needed to come out, but now that they have, I feel purged of anger. "I'm sorry, Fick. I don't want to kill anyone, either. This is some bullshit we *have* to deal with, though, so I'm dealing with it my own way. I'm sorry you had to kill Betty, but you did *have* to."

Fick doesn't say anything, but he does nod in a way that tells me he's sorry, too.

"Hey, guys?"

"Sid!" we cry, turning our attention to the voice on the other side of the room.

"Can someone tell me what the hell is going on here?" Sid replies, trying to make sense of the scene before him: three blood-soaked friends arguing around the corpses of his coworkers.

"It's a long story, buddy." I reply. "Let's talk about it back in the safety of the server room!"

CHAPTER 7
BEST-LAID PLANS

ZOOK'S PRIVATE HELICOPTER has landed, still against the backdrop of a beautiful, upstate, New York estate. Inside the study of the sprawling home, Jacobs works efficiently, setting up LCD screens, laptops, modems and telecommunications equipment. Working methodically, he powers up each piece of equipment in its proper boot sequence to assure communications will be fully functional. As systems spring into life, Jacobs makes his way to his laptop. With a couple of keystrokes, all systems are online and ready to go. He heads out of the study and down the hall to the great room. There, he approaches the back of a leather chair that sits before the fireplace. Zook sits with a glass of cognac in one hand and a smoldering cigar in the other.

"Communications are online, Mr. Zook," Jacobs reports, "and the buyers have been put on notice."

"Very good, Jacobs! You're a good soldier. When this is all done with, I'm going to have you run all operations. You're a loyal servant."

"Thank you, sir! We'll be establishing connection with the buyers at thirteen-hundred hours."

"Well done."

Zook's cell phone rings and he starts, looking down at the caller ID.

"Well, here's the call we were waiting for," Zook says, smiling. "Hello, this is Zook... Oh my God, that's terrible! Does anyone know how it happened?" He pauses as the caller briefs him on the situation. "People attacking people? That sounds terrible! Well, thank goodness we have lockdown measures in place. I hope everyone was able to get out of the building unharmed." Zook lapses into a faux-thoughtful pause, but it's overtaken by genuine shock. "What do you mean, 'the whole building'? I thought we were talking about the laboratory! I see... Well, keep me informed. I'll be there as soon as I can." Zook hangs up the phone and, with a piercing stare, engages Jacobs.

"I thought the plan was to contain the outbreak to the seventy-fifth? I was just told that the *whole damn building* is on lockdown. What happened, Jacobs?"

"I can only imagine that security staff didn't follow protocol and the perimeter was compromised."

"Well, that's just great! You know what happens now? It's only a matter of time until the whole world knows about this. Zombies running wild at Zook Towers! Hell, they might as well just call it 'Zombie Towers', now!"

"My apologies, sir. Had Zoe and her staff done their job, this wouldn't have happened."

"Zoe and her staff are either dead or mindless zombies, so yeah, you've made a great choice there, in your search for a scapegoat. Damn it, Jacobs, I can see the headline now! 'Z Towers terrorizes Manhattan with the walking dead'!"

"Yes, sir. Again, my apologies. What further course of action would you like to take?"

"Same plan as before, but now we'll need to bring in some reinforcements to control this situation of yours. The NYPD will spend too much time meddling; we need the military to take over. Call our friends at the Pentagon and bring them up to speed."

"Yes, sir!" Jacobs responds as he turns and leaves the room.

Standing on the inside of the police tape, Captain Jeffords hangs up the phone and pauses for a second, deep in thought. Staring at his phone, he makes his way to the chief, who's just finishing up a press conference.

"All we can tell you at this moment is that we have a developing situation inside Zook Towers. The interior of the building is completely locked down, and we have been unable to gain entry at this time."

"Have you made contact with anyone inside?" asks a reporter.

"Other than some nine-one-one calls, no."

"Have any terrorist organizations claimed responsibility?"

"Who said anything about terrorists?" the chief replies.

"Jim Fotz from *Channel Four News*; what can you tell us about zombies?"

"Are you trying to promote panic, Jimmy?"

"No, Chief! We've received reports of seemingly cannibalistic attacks on people in this building, and we just learned that the NYPD is currently detaining our helicopter pilot and cameraman. We're just looking for the truth."

"What, the truth about 'zombies'? Your question is too absurd to answer, and your pilot is being questioned for flying over restricted airspace during an active investigation. Now, listen carefully! I am asking all of you to be responsible with your reporting. The last thing New York needs is people panicking over absurd reports about zombies! There will be no more questions at this time."

As the chief walks away from the reporters, Captain Jeffords appears at his elbow.

"Well, now everyone in New York thinks there are zombies in the city," he says.

"I just got off the phone with Zook."

"Oh, really? What does he make of all this?"

"He reacted like anyone who was just told his building is under attack."

"Then why do I feel like you don't believe him? Speak up, Captain."

"His initial reaction was as expected, but he seemed to grow more anxious when I told him the whole building was under lockdown. Until then, he believed I was only talking about the laboratory."

"And?"

"I never mentioned the lab, sir. It seemed like a strange assumption."

The chief ponders for a moment and then replies, "Get me everything you have on Zook Labs! I want to know exactly what they do there and exactly who they do it for."

"On it, Chief."

"And find me someone inside that building I can talk to! There must be someone holed up somewhere that can give us an inside view of what's going on. We need eyes on the inside!"

"Yes, sir."

CHAPTER 8
WHAT'S HAPPENING?

"SID, DID YOU get the PBX system up, yet?"

"Working on it now, Tyson."

Power was restored to the building some time ago, but with all the turmoil over saving Sid, it took a while for us to think about bringing the systems back online. Our first objective is to restore the phone system, and then we intend to work on hacking back into the security cameras, since they rebooted and kicked us out. I know security cameras should be our first logical choice, since it will give us a good idea of just how screwed we are, but after what we went through with Justin and Betty, no one is eager to see the massacre that awaits us. We know we have to look at some point, but wallowing in denial for a little while won't kill us. At least, I hope it won't. To be honest, it's the waiting, the not knowing, that's killing us. We've been locked in this room for hours with no contact, not a single person reaching out to us. Getting the systems back online will at least give us a glimpse of life outside these walls. If it doesn't, it'll at least reveal what our options are. Then, the waiting will be over, and we can work on a game plan.

"Yes!" Sid exclaims. "The phones are back online! Who do you want to call first?"

Tyson responds, "I don't know, how about we order a pizza? Wait, before we do that, maybe we should call nine-one-one to see what the hell is going on here!"

"Right! Nine-one-one makes sense. Calling now on speaker phone…"

An older woman with a Brooklyn accent answers the phone.

"Nine-one-one, what's your emergency?"

"Hello, my name is Sid, I work at Zook Towers. Me and my friends are locked in the server room on the fiftieth floor."

"What's your emergency?"

"Well, thought you may have heard by now, but the building is overrun with zombies. You know, the kind that eat your *fucking brains!* It would be great to get some help in here!"

"Sir, please calm down. I'm going to place you on hold."

The operator's voice is suddenly replaced with Kenny G music.

"They put me on hold… *with Kenny G!*"

"Gloria!" The nine-one-one operator hollers. "I have some guy on the phone who says Zook Towers has been overrun by zombies!"

Gloria scrambles by with a sergeant close in tow.

"Patch the call through to my office!" she exclaims, signaling to her supervisory office down the darkly lit call center, "and keep your voice down. We don't want to start a panic!"

"You telling me there's zombies in the city?" the operator asks, popping her gum.

"I'm telling you to keep your voice down until we figure out what's going on down at Zook Towers! You know the entire building is on lockdown and the calls that were coming in were frantic screams. This is the first caller that's actually *talking*."

"Alright, alright! The call is waiting for you on line three."

"Hello, this is nine-one-one, Supervisor Gloria speaking, you're on the call with Sergeant O'Malley from the NYPD. Can you tell us your name, how you are doing and what's going on inside your building?"

"I can tell you that your hold music sucks balls," Sid spits, clearly distraught and probably not the best person to lead the call at this point, "and who puts someone in the middle of a zombie outbreak on hold?"

"Sid, Sid, I got this," I murmur, rubbing his shoulders and gently taking control of the phone. "Hello, Gloria, my name is Tyson. Please excuse my friend Sid; we've been locked up here in the server room for hours with no information, not to mention no food, water or bathroom breaks. To answer your question, we're currently doing fine and, to be frank, we have no idea what's going on in the building."

"How many are with you, right now?"

"It's me, Sid and my friends Johnny and Fickle. We're currently holed up in the server room on the fiftieth floor. It's secure right now, but we haven't ventured out too far to see just how safe."

"What makes you think you're in danger? Sid mentioned zombies."

"Well, I was hoping you knew more than we do, but that doesn't sound like it's the case. We had an alarm go off, and suddenly we were locked in the server room. It's designed to lock when a security protocol is initiated. When power was restored, we were able to get out. That's when we saw Sid and two coworkers who looked like they wanted to eat him."

"Where was Sid coming from?"

"He was locked in the maintenance closet."

"Why?"

"That's irrelevant to the current situation," I say, noticing Sid's growing discomfort.

"You mentioned they looked like they wanted to eat him, what do you mean by that?"

"Ever see *Zombieland*?"

"No."

"*Night of the Living Dead*?"

"Sorry!"

"Jesus! Well, imagine a zombie and then imagine said zombie trying to bite your fucking face off. Something like that!"

"Tyson, this is Sergeant O'Malley. I understand. Where are these coworkers now?"

"Well, they're dead now."

"And how did that happen?"

"Well… Wait! Do I need to get my lawyer on the phone?"

"Not necessary, Tyson. Do me a favor and just hold for a few seconds. Captain Jeffords is on the scene, I'm going to transfer you."

CHAPTER 9
EMERGENCY RESPONSE

"HELLO, THIS IS Captain Jeffords, who am I speaking to?"

"This is Tyson, I'm inside Zook Towers."

Captain Jeffords pauses for a moment, covers the mouthpiece of the phone and scrambles over to the chief.

"Chief, I have a Tyson on the phone. He says he's calling from inside Zook Towers."

"Come with me," says the chief, looking anxious. They make their way inside a secure police communication RV.

"Everyone out!" the chief exclaims. Three men and one woman take off their headsets and hastily exit the vehicle.

"Tyson," the chief says into the phone, "this is Chief Franklin from the NYPD; tell me exactly where you are and your current situation."

"Oh, hey Chief! Hey, guys, I have the chief of the NYPD on the phone! I'd say that proves our situation is pretty fucked."

"Calm down, Tyson. Please tell me all you can."

"Well, Chief, me and three of my boys are currently locked in the server room on the fiftieth floor. I'd say the current situation is pretty dire, since it seems that everyone outside of this server room is a face-eating zombie. To be honest, I was hoping you could tell me what the hell is going on, not the other way around!"

"Listen, I understand you're upset—"

"Upset? I had to beat my coworker's head with a paper cutter until his brain looked like a sloppy joe sandwich. To make matters worse, you're asking me what I know, which tells me you guys don't know jack shit! Yeah, I guess I would say that I'm pretty upset."

"Listen, I'm gonna need you to calm down so we can help you!"

Taking a deep breath, I say, "Okay, now I'm calm, what would you like to know?"

"You mentioned that you have three people with you; is everyone okay?"

"Oh yes, we're great." I say sarcastically

"Okay, can you describe your current situation?"

"We're currently in the server room on the fiftieth floor. We have AC, power and a phone. We also have a peephole in our server room door to see the immediate outside offices. Currently, there are two hacked-up zombies in our sightline that used to be our coworkers. That's about it! So, when can you come get us?"

"We're working on a plan. For now, sit tight and don't open that door."

"Chief," Captain Jeffords says insistently.

"What is it, Jeffords?" replies the chief, covering the mouthpiece.

"The army just rolled up on the scene, and when I say 'rolled up', I mean it looks like the entire army just arrived."

The chief opens the door of the RV to see two dozen convoy trucks of military personnel pulling up, accompanied by a dozen black SUVs. Overhead, six apache helicopters buzz into view.

"Jesus!" The chief shakes his head, then takes his eyes off the sky, getting back to his call. "Alright, listen to me, Tyson: I have your number here and will call you back with extraction instructions. In the meantime, don't leave that room. You're safest there."

"Wait, when are you going to call me back?"

"As soon as we finalize our plan. Do me a favor, don't talk to anyone else. You're to work with the NYPD only, at this point. You have to trust me on this. Until we reconnect, sit tight!"

"Well, that'll be... Hello? *Hello?* He hung up on me!"

"So what's the bet?" Vegas chimes.

"The bet is to sit tight, trust no one and wait for further instructions."

The chief walks out of the RV with a small entourage of officers on his flank. As he walks towards the endless line of military vehicles, he's approached by a high-ranking soldier with his own flanking entourage.

"I'm Chief Franklin of the NYPD," the chief insists, "and I have control and jurisdiction of this crime scene."

"Not anymore, we're taking over," says the official in the middle of the pack.

"Sergeant Braxton," growls Chief Franklin, looking down at the name badge before him. "Under what authority?"

"Under the authority of the president of the United States. And it's Sergeant *Major* Braxton. You and your men are to confine yourselves to perimeter duty and crowd control."

"The situation is currently under control. You can't just take over!"

"I assure you, I can. I need a complete briefing on what's going on inside the building, and you can provide that while the rest of your men hop on a horse and hold the goddamn line. Martial law is now in effect."

"Martial law? Isn't that a bit extreme for a locked-down building that we clearly have control of? What exactly is going on here, Sergeant Major?"

"That information is on a 'need to know' basis. All I need to know from you now is whether you're willing to cooperate with us or whether you need to be removed."

The chief is ready to argue, but he sees two heavily armed Humvees joining the garrison of military personnel.

"You have our full cooperation," he says.

"Good. Now, what can you tell me about this building? Have you made contact with anyone inside?"

"This is Zook Towers; you may have heard of the owner. He's the billionaire responsible for supplying you with most of your weapons, here. He's not inside, though; he's out of the office. We talked to him a while ago. Seemed concerned about the wellbeing of his employees."

"Anyone make contact with anyone on the inside?"

The chief pauses for a second.

"Nope."

"Are you sure about that, Chief?"

"Yes, Sergeant Major. Not for lack of trying. Seems like all comms are down within the building. Almost like a security protocol completely took the building off the grid."

"Anything else?"

"That's all I can think of at the moment. If anything else pops into my head, you'll be the first to know."

"Okay, now, if you could kindly draw your men back, we will take it from here."

"Jeffords, tell the men in blue to stand down. Martial law is now in effect."

Looking dejected, Jeffords responds, "Yes, sir."

"Chief, what gives?" Jeffords exclaims as they make their way away from the military personnel.

"There's a lot more going on here than a terrorist event. My money is on something shady with the military and Zook. Think about it; martial law on a completely contained crime scene! I know how the military works, and this is way outside protocol. I'm not sure exactly what's going on here, but I know the smell of bullshit. Something tells me the sergeant major isn't too concerned with the wellbeing of anyone in that building."

"Why didn't you tell him we have someone on the inside?"

"Think about it, Jeffords. These guys aren't here to control the situation. Look at the arsenal they brought along. They might be here to protect something inside that building, or to make sure nothing comes out of it, but they're not concerned with getting New Yorkers to safety. With Zook and his shady business practices, who knows their real intent? All I know is that they'll try to remove us from the situation if they can. We need to make sure that doesn't happen. You understand what I'm saying, Jeffords?"

"Yes, sir. I think you're telling me to ignore direct orders from a high-ranking military officer, risk my career, my pension and possible jail time in an attempt to save a few New Yorkers."

"That's right. You in?"

"Um, hell yeah, I'm in! What's the plan?"

"I'm working on it."

CHAPTER 10
BACK ONLINE

'M GOING OUT of my damn mind locked in this server room. It's so funny that just a few short hours ago, this was my solace, my place of zen. Now, it's my prison. The walls are closing in on me and, worse, I can't handle Fickle rocking and whining, Sid banging away on the KVM keyboard and Vegas constantly telling us what our odds for survival are. Only a few hours in, and I'm ready to commit murder because I'm so freaking annoyed! I guess that's how fast shit can fall apart. It's like my own adult version of *Lord of the Flies*.

"Hey, guys," Sid screeches, "you're all gonna want to suck my dick when I tell you what I just did!"

"Probably not, but let's see," I say, making my way to the server rack, where Sid has been pecking at the keyboard.

"I just got all the video cameras back online!"

"You're kidding me!" I exclaim, looking over to see all the monitors light up with video surveillance. Vegas makes his way over while Fickle continues to pout in the corner.

"Fickle," I shout, "get over here and suck Sid's dick for being a genius!"

Fickle rises slowly, motivated solely by morbid curiosity

about what lies outside our prison walls. We all take a moment to observe the spectacle of dead bodies, gory, blood-soaked hallways and seemingly hundreds of mindless zombies slumbering in the offices and halls of our building. All is silent, except for Sid gleefully banging away at the keyboard. Sid's a good friend of mind, mostly because he has no real friends. He has a genius IQ, but he's completely devoid of emotion. He doesn't understand innuendos or mockery, takes everything at face value. Sure, he's infatuated with Susie, but only because she's teased him for years. Stupid bitch is probably a zombie now.

"I have another surprise for you, Tyson," says Sid, a shit-eating grin spreading across his face.

"Well, the best I can do is to have Fickle add a rimjob to his blow."

"The network may be back up, but the internal firewalls are down."

"So?"

"So I can get to any camera in the building now, including your girlfriend's."

I hadn't mentioned it because I didn't want to be a whiny bitch like Fick, but I'd been struggling to come to terms with Zoe's fate. Sid's comment has me terrified to even look. Surely he wouldn't tell me about this unless Zoe was okay? Then again, it's Sid. He's not capable of understanding how seeing her dead, or as a zombie, would impact me emotionally.

"Sid, don't screw with me."

"I'm not. Do you want to see her?"

"Is she dead?"

"Take a look," he says breezily, pulling up the feed on the main monitor. There she is, locked in a security office. I move towards the screen, just to make sure my eyes aren't deceiving me. She's alive! I can't believe what I'm seeing; she has her head down, scared, but she's alive! As I walk a little closer, she lifts her head off the desk. Her eyes are red, she's been crying. Guessing that this whole outbreak started on her floor, I can only imagine what she's been through. I walk closer and touch the screen under her eyes, as if to wipe away the tears. Suddenly, I'm overwhelmed with emotion.

"We have to get to her! We have to save her!"

"Yeah, that's not going to happen," a suddenly engaged Fickle replies. "Going to ground zero to try and save a girl you've only talked to in an elevator is the dumbest shit I've heard since this outbreak happened."

"Screw you, Fick! You're such a wuss."

"Well, a wuss I may be, but at least I'm not a moron. Sid, pull up the camera in the suite outside Ty's girlfriend's office."

Sid starts searching through the hundreds of camera IP addresses, trying to decipher the adjacent cameras.

"Here they are," he says, pulling them up. "Take a good look, Tyson. That place is crawling with hundreds of goddamn zombies! We nearly got our asses kicked by *two* of them, and one was a frail-ass woman who could barely lift a coffee pot. Now, you want us all to risk our lives so you can be a hero and maybe get a hook-up out of it? I say, 'no thanks'."

"He's right, Tyson," Vegas chimes in. "The odds are really against us."

I know they're right, but shit, we've been locked up in this server room, helpless and hopeless. Suddenly, I feel like I have some purpose, and these pussies would rather sit and die in this room than do something meaningful.

"Plus, how do you even know she isn't behind this outbreak?" Fickle demands.

"Screw you, Fick! She's up there crying and scared, and you think she's a conspirator in the apocalypse! Go to hell, man. Go to hell."

"All I'm saying is that she works as security detail in a lab we all know does crazy shit, and now this happens. We're staying put and waiting for the cops."

"You wait, you asshole. *You* didn't talk to those cops, I did. They have no damn clue what's going on. Think about this: what are the chances we even get out of here alive? They probably want everyone in the building dead. We need to start thinking about our own plan, instead of just waiting for someone to save us. No one's coming! I think we need to form our own plan, who's with me?"

"I'm in" Sid says without hesitation.

"Fick, Vegas?"

"I'll help you with the plan, but no guarantees," Vegas says.

"Fick?"

"Go screw yourself! It's just like you to rally the troops when it's for your personal gain." He looks to Sid and Vegas. "You're so keen to help him look like a goddamn hero, but it'll probably get you both killed."

"Fick, listen to me," I say. "Just hear the plan and then decide. I guess it comes down to a simple choice, really. Get busy living or get busy dying."

"Did you just quote *The Shawshank Redemption?*"

"I know you love that movie."

"Fine! I'll hear your plan."

"Yes! Well, I don't have one yet, but I have some ideas."

CHAPTER 11
ZOMBIES FOR SALE

"WHO DO WE have online, Jacobs?" Zook asks, chewing on the end of an unlit Cuban cigar.

"We have representatives from twenty-five allied nations, including Saudi Arabia, Israel, a few European countries and Russia. I know they're not technically an ally, but considering your dealings in Russia, I figured you'd approve. They're all waiting for the bidding to start."

"Good work, and good call adding Russia. We know they have lots of money and a mutual interest. Our current president is too much of a pussy to make a ballsy call like this, but I'm not. Radical Islam *will* fall."

"You're a true patriot, sir," Jacobs responds.

"I know. In fact, I'm probably the last real patriot in this country. I'm probably more of an American patriot than Abe Lincoln or Ronald Reagan. I'll show them how a real man fixes things."

"We're ready to start the bidding, sir."

"Good, put me on. Make sure you cloak my identity and change my voice."

Jacobs launches the secure video feed with a blurred close-up of Zook, masking his identity. He signals a countdown, '3,2,1…'.

"Good afternoon. As you know, we have a biological agent that has the tremendous capability to take out an entire evil country in mere days. Like you, we're interested in stamping out terror across the globe. America has been pussified to a point that they're content with mass killings, bombings and shootings because our friends in Washington are too afraid of offending terrorists. Well, I stand before you as our forefathers did, standing against our government in the name of patriotism, and I am asking you, our friends, to stand up as well, to take our world back from fear. I have a solution to deal with terrorist cowards, but I need a partner who isn't afraid to get a little blood on their hands. Someone who understands an iron fist is the best approach to a psychotic enemy, and someone who can keep this transaction confidential. Bidding starts at five billion dollars!"

Jacobs kills the video feed and types in the starting bid. Bidding is instantaneous, jumping in increments of billions until it evens out at the highest bid: forty-five billion dollars. Zook raises the cigar to his mouth, lights it up and blows a huge plume of smoke as a sinister smile spreads across his face.

"Congratulations, sir," Jacobs responds. "You just doubled your net worth in less than five minutes."

"Make the arrangements and let me know when the wire transfer clears."

"Do you want to know who won the bid?"

"It doesn't matter. We're all on the same side, after all."

CHAPTER 12
BABY STEPS

BEING LOCKED UP in this room was agony even before I knew Zoe was alive, but now it's pure torture. I have Sid working overtime trying to find a contact number for the room she's in. Even though the firewalls are down, giving us access to the video feed, the phones aren't listed anywhere. Poor Sid has called at least five hundred numbers so far, to no avail. I'm trying to keep my cool; letting myself explode would only pressure Sid too much and freak out the others. It's going to be hard to talk these guys into coming with me to save Zoe, and I'm starting to think we need a few small wins to build their confidence. Time to get to work.

"Hey guys, I think it's time to gather some supplies, food and weapons."

"If that means leaving the security of this room, I'm out," Fick snaps.

"Hear me out! We have the video feed, now."

"So?"

"So, let's use it to our advantage. We can recon the areas with known supplies. Sid, bring up all the cameras on this floor."

Sid does as I ask, and while zombies are swarming over the

majority of the floor, I can undoubtedly see some areas that are clear.

"Okay, look. From where we are, there's a clear path to the break room, the office supply closet and the maintenance room. Here's the plan. Sid, you go to the break room to gather food and water."

"Got it!" Sid replies.

"Vegas, you hit the office supply closet. You're looking for anything that can be used as a weapon. You're looking for sharp objects or anything heavy and blunt."

"Like what, a staple gun?"

"I don't know, man. Channel your inner MacGyver and figure it out."

"Okay."

"I'll go to the maintenance room. I'm sure I can find some supplies there."

"What about me?" Fickle responds, almost disappointed not to be part of the plan.

"You stay here and keep an eye on the video. Let us back in after we're done."

"Well, that sucks!"

"Listen, I'm being real here. You're acting like a huge wuss, and the last thing I need is to have to save you because you don't have the balls to do what's necessary. Stay here and let us back in. Got it?"

"Fine!" Fick yells. He had to throw up a protest to prove that he has at least one nut in his sack, but it wasn't a fight he wanted to win. I can tell he prefers to sit around and wait for someone to save him, rather than try to help himself in any way. No wonder he's locked into middle management; he's incapable of making the hard calls.

"Alright, everyone understand what they're doing?" I ask, getting a series of head bobs as everyone quietly picks up their weapons. Fick makes his way to the server room door, gazes out the peephole and slowly opens the door. We all take a couple of deep breaths and make our way out of the room, but Betty and Justin's corpses still knock us back on our heels. Being locked in the server room watching from a distance gave it a sense of make believe. Seeing their limp, lifeless bodies is a reminder of just how serious our situation is.

"Okay, guys, remember your mission. See you back here in ten minutes."

Vegas and I clearly grasp the magnitude of the situation, but Sid seems almost giddy. We set off in our respective directions while Fickle slowly closes the door behind us.

"Good luck," he whispers.

CHAPTER 13
SUPPLIES

VEGAS AND SID are off on their way. Johnny is by no means a killer, but I have faith that, when push comes to shove, he can do what needs to be done. I'm less worried about Sid. Not that Sid's a maniac, but he won't hesitate to bash someone's head in. Both the office supply closet and the break room are close to the server room, so I'm guessing they'll be back before me. The maintenance room is on the other side of the suite, and definitely the riskier run, but if I want to instill confidence, I need to show I'm willing to take risks. It's also a blind spot for the cameras, so we couldn't scope it out first. Sid's run to get food and water is just to keep him busy, since it's only been five or six hours, and I don't expect Vegas to find much in the supply closet. I mean, what office supplies could he possibly collect that could be used to kill zombies? Still, giving them a mission means giving them a purpose. All I need is for them to come back safe, and then we can start working on something of a bit more consequence.

It's not long before I'm completely on my own, nearly over-whelmed by fear but amped-up with exhilaration. I have no idea what to expect in the maintenance room, but I know I can run back to safety. In the meantime, I'm considering the 'how' of actually reaching Zoe. The others aren't up to that kind of mission yet, but eventually they'll start asking questions. I need to work up some answers before they can even ask their questions. I feel like I have Sid on my side, but Vegas and Fick are clearly not onboard. Well, Fick is a huge liability anyway, but I need Vegas, and I feel like they're a package deal at this point. Hopefully, Fick can get past this nervous breakdown and nut up.

As I slowly make my way to the maintenance door, I realize that I don't have a key. I quietly jiggle the handle and, sure enough, it's locked. Maybe I can jimmy it. I pull off my ID badge and attempt to wiggle it between the door frame and the latch, but there's no hope. I kick the door in complete frustration. It rattles, and there's an answering grunt from down the hall. A figure shuffles around the corner; a terrifying silhouette, but one I know. It's Glen, the guy who liked to eat chips in my ear while I tried to fix his computer.

"Glen?" I whisper, hoping he's just injured. He lumbers a few more steps and we both come to a realization. For me, it's that he's a damn zombie. For him, it's that he just found something to eat. He starts to run at me, and I take a fighting stance, not even considering running away. I'm not sure if it's because I have the 'fight over flight' gene, or because I've had the fantasy of bashing in Glen's fat, chip-eating face for years. Whichever it is, the closer he gets, the more amped-up I get to stab him in the skull. For a fat dude, he's moving fast, though. Too fast! He lunges at me at almost superhuman speed, and I barely have a chance to catch him with the paper cutter. He lumbers away as I reposition myself for the next blow, but when he looks up at me, I realize the magnitude of what's happening. Not just with Glen, but with this whole zombie attack. His eyes are completely devoid of human life. Sadness for humanity starts to creep into my thoughts as I gaze deeper into Glen's lifeless, gray eyes. Obnoxiously eating a bag of chips in my ear doesn't seem to merit having his head bashed in, anymore. Before this, yes, I dreamed about choking the life out of the guy, but now I feel sorry for him. Perhaps this is what Fickle feels like all the time. Poor bastard. Maybe I've been too hard on him. As I continue to look at Glen, he rounds on me, and I realize I need to snap out of it. His eyes show sadness, but his mouth says the Tyson buffet is open for business. I raise my weapon over my head and bring it down, right between his eyes. He freezes, motionless, but his eyes pierce my own. That was nowhere near satisfying, but it was completely necessary. That's the real difference between me and Fick; I'm capable of doing what's necessary, but he'd prefer everyone else do the heavy lifting. That's why he's stuck in a dead-end position and will never be considered for promotion: no balls.

As I try to remove my cutter from Glen's skull, I realize it's completely stuck. Man, I really jacked it in there. I put my foot on his face and give a couple good pulls. Damn! As I struggle, I hear a noise from down the hall. Three more zombies have made their way to my location. I look the other way and see two more. I guess my racket attracted their attention.

"Let go, Glen, you fat-ass!" I shout, realizing I don't really have that 'fight over flight' gene, because I want to run so bad right now. Unfortunately, Glen has my weapon, and my only way out is to get past these zombies. After a couple of sways back and forth, I can feel the machete loosening, and finally it gives. It's not before time, because they're in a full-fledged sprint, now. I'm pretty sure this is it for me. I can't fight all of them, and I don't have anywhere to run. I turn my attention back to the maintenance door. It's my only chance, so I kick out frantically, but the door won't give a damn inch, no matter how hard I throw my weight at it. It'll be over soon. I turn back to the zombies to make my final stand. Just as I start to raise my cutter, the maintenance door slams open and someone grabs me by the shoulders and drags me into the room. The door is hurled closed and the room falls dark; I can only see a silhouette of a man standing over me. My heart is pounding through my chest in fear as he leans in, but I've started to make out his face. It's a guy I recognize from the building; a facilities worker, I think, who never talks to anyone and mostly keeps his head down.

He puts out his hand to help me up and says, "Welcome to the apocalypse!"

CHAPTER 14
SID'S HOOK-UP

S ID PEEKS INTO the break room, whispering 'hello' to see if anyone's around. He's armed with a table leg; a nice, blunt weapon for bashing in heads. After taking some small steps into the room, he realizes he's definitely all alone. Growing in confidence, he puts down his weapon on the break room table and meanders to the fridge. He looks in to find several leftover options, but nothing that looks too reliable. He opens a container of Chinese food, gives it a big sniff and nearly vomits from the smell.

"Gross!"

The rest of the containers are clearly marked 'Do not eat', so he closes the fridge in frustration.

"Nothing!"

He begins rifling through the cabinets, only to find dishes, glasses and various spices. Looking disappointed, he steps back, glancing around until he notices the vending machine.

"Pay dirt!" he chuckles, walking up to the vending machine. Pulling out his wallet, he suddenly realizes he has no small bills.

"Dang! I need some ones."

Meanwhile, back in the server room, Fickle is watching Sid on the security monitor.

"That dumbass is trying to pay!" he says aloud. "Just break it, you stupid idiot! Wait... What are you *doing?*"

Sid looks around and sees his table leg sitting on the table. He picks it up and makes his way back to the vending machine, grinning like a lunatic. He takes a step back, gets into a Jedi fighting stance and goes into a choreographed light saber ritual that would make any *Star Wars* nerd proud, swinging wildly around the room while making noises with his mouth. Suitably pumped-up, he refocuses his attention on the vending machine, does a three hundred and sixty degree spin and *SMASH!*, shatters the glass front. Reveling in success, he bows low and then holsters his weapon. Honor satisfied, he puts his table leg down on the counter and starts searching for a bag in which he can gather up his loot. He finds some grocery bags in a cabinet and makes his way back to the vending machine. As he starts to fill his bag, a presence makes its way into the door frame of the break area. Sensing he's not alone, he slowly turns his head to see who's there.

"Susie?" he says to the woman in the doorway. "Oh, thank God!"

"Sid, what are you doing?" Fickle cries, covering his mouth in horror. "Run! Fight! Don't just stand there!" He watches, helpless, as Susie lunges at Sid. "Holy shit, Sid! Get out of there before she kills you!"

Sid puts his hands up as Susie tackles him. His head ricochets off the ground and the world goes fuzzy. He's having trouble thinking clearly.

"What are you doing?" he says. "Don't worry, I'm not going to hurt you!"

Susie looks down at him with her beautiful doe eyes, and he realizes dimly that they have a slight gray tint that he's never noticed before. It's as if she's trying to say she's sorry.

"I'm so mad at you, Susie. You really hurt me today!"

Susie pulls away, clearly ashamed, but then thinks better of it. In a flurry of passion, she leans in to kiss his neck.

"Now you want me?" he says furiously, pushing her away. "Now that I'm probably the last man alive?"

Fickle watches in agony as what used to be his coworker Susie attempts to chew Sid's face off. Every time she darts forwards, he thinks she's going to connect, but Sid is managing to keep her at bay. The trouble is, he's making no real attempt to get away.

"Come on, Sid! Get out of there!"

Susie is being so insistent, and Sid has to admit to himself that he's getting aroused. More than anything, though, he feels confused, dizzy even, and that isn't how he wants this; he wants to be present, to be active in their love.

"Wait!" he shouts, needing some space, and pushes Susie back. She stumbles, uncharacteristically inelegant, and lands hard on the shredding machine in the corner of the room. As she tries to get up, her hand brushes across the top, and it whirs into life. Her scarf, carefully chosen, is sucked into the shredder, and the machine screams, chewing up the material before stalling with her face pressed right up against it.

"Yes!" Fickle exclaims, as the trapped Susie scrabbles against the shredding machine. Giving up on freedom, Susie begins to chomp in Sid's direction, still futilely trying to chew his face off.

"Now get the hell out of there!" Fickle shouts.

Lights are going off in Sid's vision, but even as his dizziness increases, he's beginning to find some clarity. Slowly, he reaches out and rubs her ass. She moans with pleasure.

"Let me take charge," he slurs, his tongue feeling oversized in his mouth. "God, your ass feels just as I imagined."

She begins to speak, but Sid remembers that morning's humiliation. He doesn't want anything to ruin the moment.

"No!" he says. "Don't speak. Just let me take charge."

He bends down, working his hands to the bottom of Susie's skirt, and then slowly makes his way up her leg, exposing everything on the way.

"Oh my god, I can't believe this is happening," he says.

"Oh my god, I can't believe this is happening!" says Fickle. It's like a car accident, and he just can't peel his eyes away. On the screen, Sid suddenly and very excitedly pulls down the zombie's panties. In a few, swift moves, he unbuckles his belt, unbuttons, unzips and drops his pants and underwear to the floor. He attempts to lunge in, but quickly realizes he isn't tall enough for easy insertion. Fickle shakes his head as his friend runs over to the cabinets and grabs a handful of porcelain plates. He makes two even stacks behind Susie, and then steps forward, climbing on top with precarious balance. A quick lunge sends the plates slipping out from under him, and he falls hard on his back, shattering them under his weight. He lays unconscious for about twenty seconds.

"Jesus," breathes Fickle.

Sid gets back to his feet, showing no sign that he knows any time has passed. He stumbles a little, vision dimming, and then runs, flailing, to the cabinets and starts ransacking them. He pulls out two family-sized coffee cans. One is Folgers and one Maxwell House. He contemplates which will better serve his task.

"'The best part of waking up is Folgers in your cup' or 'good to the last drop'?" he sings. "This seems like a 'good to the last drop' moment. Screw you, Folgers, I'm going with Maxwell House!"

He puts the can behind Susie and hops on top. He now has the perfect height and balance to make it happen. He takes a deep breath and thrusts inside Susie. She shrieks in pleasure.

"Stop talking!" Sid blurts out, grinning as he looks up in pure, thrusting elation.

Fickle raises his head out of the garbage can next to him, looks at the monitor and then turns squeamish again. He slams his head back into the garbage can and resumes vomiting.

Twenty minutes later, Vegas enters the break room. He sees Sid sitting at the table with a huge pile of snacks from the vending machine. Sid is positively glowing, chowing down on junk food, but the room is wrecked. Vegas looks around, taking in the broken plates, the glass, the ransacked vending machine, the crumpled coffee can and, of course, the stranded, panty-less zombie frantically chomping at him. He thinks for a minute, trying to put together a sensible timeline to explain the scene, but nothing occurs to him.

"What the hell, Sid!" he says eventually. "Did you eat all the damn Zingers?"

CHAPTER 15
MEETING MATT

"**T**HANKS MAN," I say, "I was about to be chopped meat out there."

"Yep," says my new best friend. "You're lucky I let you in."

With his help, I stand and look around the place. It's a huge room full of workbenches, tools and equipment; plenty of great materials for a new weapon. Hell, a big-ass monkey wrench is all I need. After my near-death experience, I'm realizing that a make-shift machete/paper cutter isn't my best option. As I get my bearings, my attention turns back to the door. I can hear the zombies clawing and moaning just outside.

"Don't worry about those guys," he says. "They'll lose interest once your scent dissipates from the hallway."

"How do you know?"

"Man, I know a lot! Especially about zombies."

I'm strangely intrigued by this guy. He comes off as being full of shit, but he has a confidence about him that makes me want to ask him more.

"Hey, I'm Tyson," I say, reaching out my hand. He stares at it, then pulls a rag out of his back pocket and proceeds to wipe his hands with no intention of extending the same courtesy. He's strong, about 6'2" and looks like he can take care of himself. The last thing I want to do is start shit, so I pull my hand back, wiping it on my pant leg.

"Anyway, thanks for saving my ass out there. I've killed a couple of them so far, but five would have been a bit much."

I'm hoping that will give me enough street cred to garner a bit of respect and keep me safe.

"I bet you think you're a badass, now?" he says smugly, making his way to one of the workbenches.

"Well, I'm not a pussy, I can tell you that!"

"We'll see," he says, reaching under the workbench to a mini-fridge. He pulls out a twelve-ounce Budweiser and tosses it to me. Not wanting to disappoint, I snap it open, suck the foam off the top and take three giant swigs. To be honest, I could have downed the whole thing. The sweet nectar is just what I need to calm the hell down. I'm trying to keep cool, but I'm still pretty ramped up.

"Name's Matt, but you can call me 'Jesus', because I'm here to save your ass."

"Hey, Matt. So, tell me—"

"I *said* you call me 'Jesus'!"

"You're serious about that?"

"Dead serious," he barks, his eyes piercing right through my soul.

"Uh, okay, Jesus… How long have—"

"Dude, I'm just messing with you! Don't call me Jesus. *Hahaha!* I mean, do I look like some sort of Jesus freak?"

"No, you don't look like a Jesus freak," I laugh, internally debating whether I should have just taken my chances with the zombies.

"Well, I very much believe in our lord and savior, Jesus Christ, so in your eyes, I guess I *am* a Jesus freak! The thing about Jesus is you can't believe in God without believing the other side exists as well."

"You mean…" I ask, swigging my beer and pointing my finger down.

"That's right, good ol' Lucifer himself. Except he doesn't live down there. He resides on the hundredth floor of this building."

"Zook?" I ask cautiously.

"Yes, Zook!" he says, matter-of-fact. "What do you think's happening here? Do you think that *Jesus* started this bullshit? Think, Tyson! Where do you think this started?"

"The seventy-fifth floor?" I guess.

"There you go!" he says, walking over and poking my head. "That's using your lumpy noggin!"

I'm trying not to get too frazzled, but Matt's starting to come off as a complete lunatic. I refocus; he seems crazy, but he also seems like he knows a hell of a lot more than I do. I mean, we all know there's some shady shit that happens on the seventy-fifth floor, and we all know Zook earned his billions by selling out humankind. I decide to press on.

"You telling me Zook had something to do with the outbreak?"

"Look who's catching up! Try to keep up with this next part," he quips, pulling out another frosty beer. "Zook's been developing a biological weapon that can turn entire civilizations into braindead zombies."

"That doesn't make any sense, not even for Zook! He's driven by greed and, with everything he owns, he'd be the last one to benefit from worldwide annihilation."

"Ah, my little shit-stain, so true! But what his minions up there developed is a godforsaken mutant zombie. See, they don't just want to eat your brains, like you see in the movies. They're driven to rapidly spread their virus; if they devour you, you're lucky. The unlucky ones turn and become one of the zombie army, but here's the real beauty: the virus ends up killing its host after a day or two. So, as long as Zook can contain the spread, he can wipe out an entire country. You know, the type of country that has lots of crude oil but is surrounded by thousands of miles of desert? Actually, it's pretty genius, if you think about it."

I sit back on the bench, completely blown away. After all, it certainly sounds plausible. Zook is a xenophobic asshole, so I can totally see him not giving a damn about humanity. As long as the good ol' USA is fine, he wouldn't give a shit! Still, I'm skeptical. Matt seems like a complete lunatic.

"How do you know all this?" I ask.

"Are you serious, man? I'm maintenance in this building! You're all so quick to overlook the maintenance guys, but there isn't anything I don't know about what happens here." He reaches into a drawer and pulls out a building schematic. "I know the layout, where they keep shit, and I have access to everything. Hell, man, who do you think they call when they want to dispose of the test subjects?"

"They tested this shit?"

"Well, on poor-ass chimps, but yeah, man. Burned the hell out of them, too! I've probably disposed of over a thousand chimpanzees over the past three months. That's how I knew this was coming to a head, and that's why I prepared myself."

Feeling completely sick to my stomach, I ask, "How do you prepare yourself for something like this?"

Matt smiles and motions for me to come closer, as he walks over to a full-sized cabinet. He opens it slowly, and I stretch my head around the corner, not sure if I actually want to see what this guy has stored in there. As I look inside, I see tons of makeshift weapons that look straight out of a zombie movie. Blunt weapons, medieval-looking axes, swords and even a mace!

"Holy shit, man, where did you get all this?"

"I made them for a day like today. We'll all end up dead in the end, but at least I can have fun killing some zombies in the process."

"Wait, what makes you think we're all going to die?"

"Dude, containment is the only medicine to stop *this* virus. They're not going to let us out of here alive. No one is going to take that chance. The military have probably already surrounded this building. They'll sit outside for forty-eight hours and then come in here with flamethrowers to burn everyone, and I mean *everyone*. I figure, while I'm still here, I may as well kill some of these zombies! You know, strike some of God's will into them, show Him I'm no pussy."

"Hell no, screw that!" I shout. "No, I'm not going to sit here and just wait to die!"

"Boy, I don't think you heard me. You don't have a choice, here."

"Bullshit! I make my own choices and I choose to live, and so will my friends! I have a plan, and you're going to help me."

"Listen here—"

"No, you listen to *me!*" I retort. Knowing you no longer have control of your destiny apparently grows you balls, because suddenly I have zero fear about Matt. "I have a plan to get out of here, and you're going to help me."

"I am?"

"That's right; God's will, right? Well, you'll have plenty of opportunity to kill zombies and help me and my friends turn this upside down and expose Zook for what he is!"

"Alright, friend, what you got?"

"First thing, let's collect as many of those weapons as possible. I have a badass crew in the server room that can use them. Also, grab your schematics and all the access keys you have for this building."

"It's all on swipe, buddy!" Matt says as he holds up the ID card clamped to the front pocket of his shirt. Apparently energized, he reaches below the workbench and pulls out a couple of duffel bags full of tools. He empties them onto the workbench and proceeds to fill them with the mass amount of weapons he's built over time. I snatch up the building schematics and shove them in the back of my pants, and he slides over a bag full of weapons. I search through the bag and find a baseball bat with nails hammered in. After a few swings, I'm happy with my choice, and I throw the rest of the bag over my shoulder. Meanwhile, Matt fills the second duffel bag with a couple more weapons, all equally crude. He stops for a moment, stares into the cabinet and grins, then reaches in reverentially. The weapon he pulls out is clearly his best; it's an ax on one end and a sledgehammer on the other. It looks like I could barely lift it, but Matt swings it around with relative ease. I can tell by the way he's swinging it that he put considerable time into its construction. Satisfied, he stops swinging and places it on the bench. Finally, he reaches into the mini-fridge, grabs a twelve-pack of Bud and tosses it into the duffel bag.

"In case we get thirsty," he explains.

"Right on! Let's go."

Duffel bags strapped over our shoulders, badass weapons in our hands, we make our way to the maintenance door, where we can still hear the scratching and moaning of zombies on the other side.

"You ready?" I ask. He pushes me out of the way.

"I was born ready!"

He throws the door open and slams his ax into the head of a zombie. I slide out, heading in the opposite direction, and land a perfect shot right between the eyes of the nearest zombie. As it tumbles back, I get a quick look of approval from Matt.

"Psalm two, seven to twelve," he intones, sizing up the remaining zombies. " I will declare the decree: the Lord hath said unto me, 'Thou art my son; this day have I begotten thee. Ask of me, and I shall give thee the heathen for thine inheritance, and the uttermost parts of the earth for thy possession. Thou shalt break them with a rod of iron; thou shalt dash them in pieces like a potter's vessel."

I rip the spiked end of my bat free and focus on the zombie making his way towards me. Suddenly, I feel invigorated. Not sure if it's Matt's gospel or my new purpose to take Zook down, but I'm suddenly pumped with adrenaline. As Matt continues to bellow scripture, I slowly start to smile.

"A-fucking-men!"

CHAPTER 16
TIME TO MAKE A PLAN

FICKLE OPENS THE door for Vegas and Sid. Sid's arms are overflowing with various snacks from the break room, while Vegas has a small bag of zip ties, duct tape and lots of pencils.

"Is Tyson back yet?" Vegas asks.

"No, not yet," Fickle says in a voice that indicates something else is on his mind, closing the door behind a concerned Vegas and a smirking Sid.

"Sid!" Fickle exclaims, once the door is closed. Sid turns around, arms still holding tons of junk food.

"What?" he asks, adopting the same tone of voice.

"You want to explain to me what you did in the break room?"

"Oh, you saw that?" Sid says, a smile spreading across his face.

"I saw it alright! What the hell were you thinking?"

"I was thinking, 'finally, I get a piece of ass from Susie'. Did you see me slip on the plates? Hahaha! I was a little excited in the beginning. Got my groove, though."

"Groove? You strapped her to the shredding machine and raped her! You're sick!"

"The hell I did! She... it... No, come on! Vegas, you saw her. Did she look like someone that didn't enjoy herself?"

Looking confused and a little nauseas, Vegas replies, "Sid, I saw a zombie that used to be Susie half-sucked into the shredder. Don't tell me you had sex with her?"

"That's bullshit! Look, I'm having trouble remembering but... Fick, pull the break room up on the monitor."

Fick gladly goes to the console to bring it up, finds the channel and sends the feed to the main monitor. Sid walks up to the monitor that shows Susie in the corner of the room, still in the same place he left her. He hadn't realized until now, but his vision had narrowed considerably, darkness creeping in from the edges. With a little time to recover, and the persuasion of his friends, the veil begins to lift.

"Wait..." Sid says, looking at Vegas and Fick. "Why would I leave her in there? Should we go back and save her?"

"Sid, you on drugs or something?" Vegas says.

"What are you talking about?" he asks, looking back at the screen. His vision is clearer now, and his thoughts move quicker. Still, he can't quite process what's in front of him.

"What do you see?" he asks, worry creeping into his voice.

"I see a zombie! Dude, Susie is a zombie."

Sid looks at the monitor again, but things still don't make sense. He steps closer, rubs his eyes and looks again. Something clicks. As she comes back into focus, it's clear that Susie is a zombie!

"What? That's not right! But, but—"

"Dude, you had sex with a zombie! That's messed up on so many levels."

"This can't be right!" Sid protests. "Oh my god, oh my god! What does this mean?"

"I don't know," Vegas says. "Susie was dripping with STDs before she turned into a zombie; who knows what they mutated into after she turned? Damn, man, you could be famous. The first STD contracted from a zombie."

"I don't want to be known as a zombie-fucker!" Sid cries. "Come on, guys, you can't tell anyone!"

Just then, there's a knock at the door. Vegas runs over, looks through the peephole and sees me in the company of a strange guy who's completely drenched in blood.

"It's Tyson, and he has someone with him!"

He throws the door open and the two of us strut in like a couple of badass bikers.

"Well, boys," I say. "I got some supplies and a kickass, zombie-killing reinforcement." We drop our duffel bags, letting the weapons spill out.

"Wow," Vegas says in excitement. "This is so much better than the packs of number two pencils I collected."

Fickle and Sid make their way over, and Fickle extends his hand.

"Hi, I'm Fickle."

"This is Matt," I say, "and he doesn't shake hands."

Fickle recoils and moves over to Sid, peeking into the duffel bags.

"So, what's going on here?" I ask, hoping they've had some easy victories.

Vegas blurts out, "Sid had sex with a zombie!"

"Really?" I ask. "Well, I wasn't expecting that."

"Goddammit, Vegas!" yells Sid. "I didn't want anyone else to know."

"Hey!" Matt pipes up. "God knows! Seeing that you had intercourse with a zombie, my guess is you're already on his bad side. No sense in making things worse by using his name in vain."

"Well, I'm sure there's a lot more to this interesting story," I interject, "but we have bigger things to talk about than Sid's suddenly prosperous, albeit deranged, love life. Zook is behind this outbreak, and thanks to intel from my good buddy here, we know we have less than forty-eight hours to formulate a plan, blow the lid off this thing and get the hell out of here."

The group falls silent, digesting my words. I can see hesitation in Fickle's face, but the others already seem to be considering our next steps.

While I've been fighting for my life, the outside of Zook Towers has turned into a three-ring circus. Hundreds of curious onlookers have started to gather at the NYPD barricades. There are two control center stations on the inside of the perimeter. One belongs to Sergeant Major Braxton and the army, and the other Chief Franklin and his team.

"Chief, can I talk to you over here?" Braxton yells from his location. The chief leans in to confer with Jeffords, nods and makes his way to Braxton's location.

"What can I help you with, Sergeant Major?" he responds with a smile.

"Have you or anyone on your team made contact with anyone on the inside?"

"Not yet. Our orders have been made clear: hold the line and make sure the perimeter isn't compromised."

"Then why have I just received intel informing me that you talked directly with someone on the inside?" The chief doesn't respond, just shrugging his shoulders in defiance. "Listen, Chief. No disrespect; I know you guys are doing your job, but we have a job to do too, and it requires the cooperation of the local authorities. You understand protocol, don't you?"

"Oh, yes. My team and I are in full compliance with your protocol, Sergeant Major."

"Then tell me about the conversation you had with 'Tyson'."

"I don't know what you're talking about, I'm afraid."

"Don't play with me, Chief! I have the nine-one-one transcript up to the point he was transferred to your Captain Jeffords, and I know you know about it. I also know you and he had a discussion about zombies."

"Well, if you know everything, I guess you don't need me."

"You're *very close* to not being needed. Do yourself a favor and get on my team. It's a matter of national security, and right now you and your team are close to being thrown in the stockade!"

"Anything else you need, Sergeant Major?"

"Stay close, Chief!" barks the soldier, and the chief smiles and stares straight ahead. "For now, you're dismissed."

"Sure thing," the chief responds, and he spins away from the sergeant major and starts to walk away. "Funny thing," he adds, stopping for a moment.

"What's that, Chief?"

"Intel is supposed to be bi-directional, and so far we haven't been briefed by your side of the house. When that changes, maybe we'll have a different conversation."

"Like I said, Chief," Braxton replies rigidly, "you're very close to being an expendable part of this mission. Stay close."

The chief smiles and proceeds to walk back to his group, calling to Jeffords.

"Let's take a walk."

Both men walk slowly away from the NYPD comm center.

"What's up, Chief?"

"Listen to me carefully. We're pretty close to being removed from the scene. I have a plan, but it needs to move fast, while we still have position."

"You got it. What's the plan?"

"Get Tyson on the phone!"

The small excursions have done their job, and I know I now have Matt and Sid onboard for some zombie bashing. Matt and I have a taste for it now, and Sid apparently has sex with zombies, so that dirty bastard should be up for anything. I need to say something to get Fick and Vegas on board with my plan, but the problem is that I don't have one. Maybe I need to switch tactics.

"Listen," I say, "there are no plans to save us, no plans for the cavalry to charge the building. The people out there know what this is, and their protocol is to wait it out, let the outbreak take care of things and then come in here and torch anything left standing. They're banking on us dying a cruel zombie death so they can sweep this under the rug! Do we want to just sit here and wait to die, or do we want to take charge, kick some zombie ass and get the hell out of here?"

"That sounds nice and all, but what's your plan?" Fickle asks defiantly.

"I know how to get us out of here," Matt interjects. He swaggers up to me and starts grabbing at my waist aggressively.

"What the hell are you doing?"

"Shut up, you dumbass!" he orders. "I need these."

He reaches into my waistband and pulls out the schematics of the building. He walks over to his duffel bag, grabs a Bud, cracks it open, takes a big swig and makes his way to the table.

"Zook is paranoid as hell," he explains. "Being able to leave by the door and his helicopter wasn't enough; he has another, secret way out." Opening up the schematics and flipping through the dozens of prints, he finds what he's looking for, slams it on the table and puts his burly, dirty finger on the spot he's referencing. "Here it is! It goes below the building here, and then there's a passageway that comes up on the opposite side of the block. Pops out at a closed newspaper kiosk, the cloak and dagger wannabe. Only problem is, it's only accessible from tower two, which is closed off, except through Zook's suite."

"Okay, okay," I say, excitement rising. "We can handle that. Now we're onto something!"

"So," Fickle says contentiously, "I guess we're supposed to just make our way to tower two, which you can only get to from

Zook's penthouse, which means surviving fifty floors of zombies and then somehow get into his penthouse which we have no access, only to survive maybe more zombies in Tower two and then strut across the boardwalk and pop out in the middle of NYC!"

"Well you can do that, if you want," Matt says, taking another sip of his beer and fingering his ID badge. "Me, I'll probably take Zook's elevator!"

"Hell yeah!" I exclaim. This is much better than I anticipated. There's no way Fick and Vegas will resist this plan. The only issue I have now is convincing them to make a pit stop for Zoe. There's no way I'm leaving this place without her.

"Okay, now we're talking!" I say, trying to build the energy. "Fick, Vegas, Sid, you in?"

"I'm in!" Sid responds excitedly.

"Statistically speaking, it's not the worst idea. I'm in," Vegas says, slowly raising his hand.

"Shit! says Fick, raising his hand.

"Okay, awesome!" I reply. "Alright, here's the plan. First, we need to take Zook's elevator to the seventy-fifth floor and retrieve Zoe, and then we make our way to Zook's passageway."

"Whoa! Who said anything about getting Zoe?" Fick says.

"What do you mean?" I respond. "There's no way we're going to leave her behind!"

"I'm not going to risk my life just so you can have the chance to save a girl that you barely know!" Fick retorts.

"Screw you, Fick! If we leave her behind, you're basically saying you're okay with letting her die. How the hell can you do that?"

"Bullshit!" he spits back. "This is about getting in Zoe's pants, not about saving lives. If we alter the plan, it puts us all at risk!" Fickle turns to Vegas. "Vegas, what are the odds for survival if we go up to the seventy-fifth floor to save Tyson's girlfriend?"

"I put the odds of survival at about seven percent."

"Seven percent!" Fickle echoes. "Do you really want to risk everyone's life so you can be a hero? We're all your friends, man. You willing to risk our lives for hers?"

"That's a bunch of crap, Fick, and you know it! Vegas, what are our odds of survival if we stick with Matt's plan?"

"I would say our odds of survival are about nine percent."

"Do you hear that, Fick? We're talking about a two-percent deviation! Are you really willing to let someone die, to lose a human life, for a mere two-percent bump in our chances?"

Fick freezes. He knows I'm right, any chance we have to save someone is a chance worth taking, but he's pissed that it's on my terms rather than his.

"Who the hell is 'Zoe'?" Matt asks, belching.

"I'll show you!" Sid says, and he heads over to the console. He bangs on the keyboard for a few minutes before the main monitor lights up with Zoe's video feed. Matt reaches into the duffel bag for another beer and sidles up to the monitor.

"Damn, man, she's fine as hell! You hitting that?"

"Um, no. We're just friends, but we did talk in the elevator today about going on a date."

"Well damn, man! I don't care what the odds are, if you have any chance to get into those pants, it's a chance worth taking."

"Thanks, Matt!" I say. "So we have a plan?"

"No!" Fickle shouts. "We don't have a plan, we have an idea! So… let's make a plan. I'm in!"

"That's my boy! Alright, let's work out—"

Just then, the server phone rings. For a moment, we all stare at it in shock, and then I snap out of my amazement and run to it.

"Hello?"

CHAPTER 17
NEW PLAN

THEY CROWD AROUND me as I speak on the phone, hanging on my every word.

"Yep... Okay... Yeah, we can do that... Sounds good... Sure, we can make that happen... Yep, we have a way in... Okay, hang on a sec!" I scramble for a piece of paper and pen. "Okay, go..." I start jotting down numbers. "Got it, see you on the other side." I hang up the phone, staring down at it as I digest what I've just been told.

"Who was it?" Fick asks impatiently.

"You guys aren't going to believe this! That was Captain Jeffords. Our plan has just been upgraded."

"Is someone coming to get us?" Fick asks excitedly.

"In a way, yes! Now, everyone sit while I lay out this plan."

Everyone takes a seat except for Matt. He walks over to the duffel bag to grab another beer.

"Matt, you joining us?" I ask, pulling the rolling whiteboard to the front of the table.

"Nah man, you just point me in a direction and I'll be there."

"Alright, just take it easy on the drinking! I need you at full strength."

"Shit, I'm just hydrating!"

"Fair enough, big fella."

I grab a couple of whiteboard markers and quickly draw an outline of Zook Towers.

"Okay, we're *here*," I say, putting an 'X' on the fiftieth floor of tower one. "We need to stop on the seventy-fifth floor to get Zoe. As you mentioned, though, that's ground zero for the outbreak, and we can clearly see through the video feed that a lot of zombies are on that floor. So, we look at seventy-four and seventy-six to see where there are less. We then take the stairs to seventy-five and lure them down the stairwell. Once they're a decent distance away, we jump back on Zook's elevator and make our way to the seventy-fifth. Then, we get Zoe and make our way to Zook's penthouse."

"What?" Fickle gasps. "Why?"

"Zook has a helipad, so *that's* when the NYPD will swoop in on a helicopter to pick us up!"

"Wait, I thought you said, 'no one out alive'?" Vegas says.

"Yeah, I know, but the NYPD are on our side. The military don't know anything about this."

"So, what's the number for?" Fickle asks. "You supposed to call them when we get to the top? We know the phone works here, but are you sure it works up there?"

"Ah, welcome to the show, Fick! Now you're thinking. This number isn't for a pickup call, it's for *Channel Two News*. I'm supposed to call, tell them we're trapped inside and then leak the story about Zook. If we can show that people are alive in here, then that might give us some slack with the military."

"Again, how are you supposed to call them after we leave?" Fick asks, pulling his smartphone out of his pocket. "It looks like our phones are still useless."

"Yeah, Jeffords thinks the military is jamming the cell signals. That, or the building is doing it, somehow. Bottom line, in an outbreak, they don't want anyone trying to contact the outside, but our phones can be used for something else. We take the cell phones, strap them to our chests, tether them to the wireless LAN and broadcast our cameras online."

"That's the dumbest thing I've ever heard," Fick says, rolling his eyes. "We still have no access to the outside world."

"That's not entirely true!" Sid pipes in. "Yes, the WAN connection is down, probably being blocked by the military, but we do have a business continuity plan that gives us an alternate path to the web."

"Don't you think the military knows that?" Fick says.

"Sure they do," Sid replies, "but do they know about the dark fiber connection that Zook had put in a few months back? You know how he likes to keep his stuff classified. We could tap into that without the military even knowing."

"Okay, great!" I say. "Now, all we need is a platform, somewhere to broadcast our stream so the whole world can see!"

"I have something," Vegas chimes in.

"What do you mean, you have something?" I ask.

"I have my gambling site!"

"Damn, man! You want to bet against our lives or something?" Fick screams out.

"Think about it, Fick," insists Vegas. "My gambling site is overseas; it isn't regulated by our government. They can't touch it, and it gets millions of hits a day! If I can get to the console, I can send a message to my admin. They'll set it all up for us!"

"I am loving this idea!" I laugh. "Sid, can you make it happen?"

"Already on it! Bringing up the dark fiber connection now... and we're up! Vegas, I need the URL for your site."

"Y-O-U-B-E-T-Y-O-A-S-S dot th" Fick replies.

"Your site is 'You bet yo' ass dot th, what is that, Thailand?" I ask.

"Hey man, all the good domains were taken."

Sid laughs, typing in the URL.

"Okay, Vegas," he says, moving away from the console, "you're up!"

"Okay, give me a couple of minutes to send a message to my admin. He's in Thailand, so we should be able to use his access without the government shutting us down."

"Fick and Matt, pull out your phones," orders Sid. "Connect to the WiFi and give me your IP addresses."

Matt and Fickle pull out their phones and start trying to connect.

"Hey," Matt responds after staring at his phone for a bit. "How do I do that stuff you just said with the WiFi, IP and all that jazz?"

"Bring it over here," Sid says. "I'll hook it up!"

Matt hands the phone to Sid, who already has his own on the table.

"How do you find your IP address?" Fickle asks.

Sid looks up and takes a quick glance at Fick and his phone.

"You have an iPhone?" Sid sighs. "How did I not know this about you?"

"What's wrong with an iPhone?" Fick responds defensively.

"Nothing, it's a very pretty phone! Unfortunately, that's it, it's otherwise useless!"

"Hey, I'll have you know that Apple owns half the market when it comes to mobile devices."

"That only means half the market is mindless. Bring your dumbass phone over here, you sheep! Even Matt has a Windows phone, and he doesn't know shit about technology. No offense Matt."

"None taken. If you ask me, you're all a bunch of dummies for knowing this technical stuff but still needing to call me to change a lightbulb."

We all laugh as Sid configures the phones.

The plan's coming together nicely, but I still don't know just how prepared we are, and I still haven't been able to find a way to make contact with Zoe. I begin to wonder if Sid can connect our laptops to the surveillance feed; that way we can constantly keep our eyes on the dangers ahead so we're not surprised. Suddenly, a brainwave; if I can see Zoe, I bet she can see us. Why didn't I think of that before? I quickly look at Zoe on the big monitor, no longer studying her, but what she's doing. I can see she has a pretty big console station with camera feeds, but of course she does! She's the main security for that floor, why wouldn't she have full access to the security equipment?

"Sid, I have a couple of requests."

"Yeah?"

"Do you think you can get the camera outside the server room to appear on Zoe's monitor?"

"I'm not sure, I'd have to get into the main controls to see if I can control all terminals." Sid walks back up to the console, standing behind Vegas, who is just finishing up.

"I'm all done here!" Vegas says, handing the keyboard over to Sid.

"Yep," says Sid, "here we go! I can have all security stations show the same feed."

"You're the best! Can you turn all stations to the video camera just outside these doors?"

"On it!"

I quickly grab a notepad and a sharpie, frantically scribbling a message. Once it's finished, I take a quick peek outside the server room door to check that it's all clear, and then step outside to get on the camera feed.

"Can you see me on the camera?" I holler.

"We see you!" Vegas shouts back. I hold up my sign, which just says 'Hi Zoe!', and hope it's appearing clearly.

"Does she see me?"

"Nope!" Sid responds. "She has her head down."

I start jumping up and down, trying anything to get her attention.

"Dude, she isn't even looking. You just look like a dumbass!" Fickle calls.

I'm not deterred, and I continue jumping up and down like a lunatic.

"She's lifting her head. Oh, she sees you! She sees you, man!"

I stop jumping like a maniac and hold up the sign.

"She sees it! 'Hi Zoe'? That's what you had to say?"

"Shut it, Vegas! What's she doing?"

"Wow, man, she's smiling! That lame-ass shit actually got her to smile! Wait, now she's looking around the room. She's digging in the drawers! What's she doing?"

"She's probably looking for something to write back on, dumbass!"

"Oh, yeah, she just pulled out a pad and she's writing on it!"

"What's it say?" I scream to Vegas in anticipation.

"It says 'Hi'! Oh my god, you guys are lame as hell! Stuck in the middle of an apocalyptic outbreak, and you guys are saying 'hi' to each other!"

"Right, get to the point, man," Fick chimes in. Now that I have her attention, I need to think of the shortest and easiest way to let her know that we're coming. I take a sec, rip off the 'Hi Zoe' note and scribble some more. I hold up the pad, which now says 'Coming to save you!'

"What's she doing?" I yell.

"She's not smiling anymore. She's writing... It says 'Save yourself!' Wait, she's writing again. It says 'Suicide mission!' She looks upset. Maybe she's right, man."

Screw that; there's no way I'm going to let her talk me out of this. She just doesn't want me to get hurt. I'd do the same, if she wanted to save me, but that's not the case. I quickly scribble some more on the pad, this time taking two sheets of paper. I hold up the first note with a smile, to put her at ease. It says 'U owe me a date'. I pause for a moment, then flip the page, which reads 'See you soon!' I quickly drop the pad and leave the camera's view to make my way back to the server room. I can see she's upset, holding up a sign that says 'No!'

"See, I told you all Tyson wants is a piece of ass," Fick says. Walking to the monitor, I can see a tear slowly running down Zoe's face. She's scared, and she needs us, but she doesn't want to put us in harm's way. I get it now, but I'm more determined than ever to get to her. I'm willing to die trying.

"Come on, guys!" I say, rallying the troops. "Of course she doesn't want us to save her; it's dangerous! But she's alone and scared and needs our help! How are you going to feel if you get out of the building alive, only to think that you left someone behind? You wouldn't be able to live with yourselves."

"Hey man, I don't blame you," Matt replies. "She's a fine piece of ass! So, what's the plan?"

"Okay, here's the plan. Everyone turn on the video cameras on your phone. Sid, lock onto each one and broadcast the stream on Johnny's site."

"On it!" Sid confirms.

"Okay, good. Our plan is to make our way to Zoe by taking the path of least resistance." I grab a Surface Pro sitting on a desk. "Can we configure this laptop to see the security cameras?"

"Easy!" Sid responds as he continues to punch away at the console keyboard.

"Good, so we'll have eyes in the sky as we make our way there. We shouldn't run into any surprises. Matt and Fick, tape your cell phones to your chests, cameras facing out."

Fick reaches into Johnny's collection of office supplies and pulls out a couple of rolls of duct tape.

"We're going to give the world a first-person perspective of what's going on here," I say, as Matt and Fick start strapping their cell phones to their chests. Sid takes a step back away from the console to get his cell phone.

"We're all set with the cameras," he says, holding up his phone to show the video perspective on the monitor. "We shouldn't all be livestreaming constantly; it'd drain the batteries really quickly, but all we have to do is hit the 'record' button when we want to show what we're seeing. Just tell me when you want me to go live."

I make my way over to the landline phone on the desk. I pull the phone number Jeffords gave me from my pocket, dial it and listen to it ring.

"*Channel Two News*, this is Mark," says a voice on the other end.

"Mark, my name is Tyson," I say, "and I'm about to win you the Pulitzer."

"Buddy, if you knew how many times I've heard that!" replies Mark, but I can tell he's smiling.

"I'm calling you from inside Zook Towers."

"You're kidding me?"

"I'm not kidding. Here's the deal; I'm going to give you a website to check out. We'll provide you live video feed of what's going on in here."

"What *is* going on?" Mark asks. "The reports we have coming in say there may be some type of terrorist attack, but our access has been completely blocked by the military."

"'Terrorist attack'? More like the end of the world! You ready for the site? We go live in five!"

"Okay, go!"

"W-W-W dot, you bet yo' ass dot th That's 'yo', Y-O."

"You serious?"

"Hey man, that's what we have to work with! That's all for now."

I hang up and start getting ready. Fickle finishes taping his phone to his chest and makes his way over to Sid, who is now working to get the Surface Pro up and running with the video feed.

"Sid," says Fickle, "you alright, man? You don't look so good."

"I'm fine!" he responds, as he continues to work on the Surface Pro.

"You don't look fine; you're sweating like a pig!"

I don't typically agree with Fick, but he's right. Sid looks like he's suddenly come down with the flu. I start to make my way over.

"I feel fine!" he protests. "I don't know if you noticed, but I'm the only one working, here! 'Sid, get the dark fiber up', 'Sid, get the Surface to pull the building cameras', 'Sid, get the cameras on the phone to live feed to Johnny's website'! Do you have any damn clue how difficult all this is?"

"Okay, okay, *relax!*" Fick responds. "Sorry!"

"Oh, and you taped your phone on backwards, you dumbass," Sid growls. "You had one thing to do, and you did it wrong!"

Fick looks down, confirming that he has indeed taped his phone on with the wrong side facing out.

"Shit!"

"iPhone users," Sid sneers.

CHAPTER 18

ZOE'S PERSPECTIVE

I SIT ALL ALONE in my room, paging through the endless camera views on the main screen while keeping one eye on the second screen, which shows the server room doors. There are streams of zombies on every floor, and in the stairwell. It's a suicide mission to try and reach me, but then we're all going to die anyway, so I guess it's better to die trying to do something than to die just waiting. There isn't much I can do to help, though. Out of all the floors with zombies, I have the biggest concentration of them, apart from the lobby. Hell, I have thirty outside my door. What a helpless feeling. I'm trained for this, I should be leading this, but instead I'm the damsel in distress. Shit! I have a man trying to save me. A nice guy who, more than likely, has no idea how to survive. Does he even have a weapon? I have plenty of firepower in my gun cabinet, but with only one finger to pull the trigger, I can't get out of here on my own. I'm smart enough to know that, so all I can do at this point is sit and wait.

"Screw this!" I exclaim, then jump up and throw open the cabinet. Every weapon I can carry, I strap to myself. I pull out a backpack, completely emptying the gun cabinet, stocking up with extra guns and ammo. I take one look back at the screen to see Tyson's note, 'See you soon'.

"Not if I see you first!"

I open the door slowly, stick the end of my machine gun with attached grenade launcher out and shoot a grenade to the center of the suite. The machine gun goes in my backpack, and I pull out twin handguns. The grenade explodes, and I throw the door open, running out to land head shot after head shot on the disoriented zombies.

CHAPTER 19

MARK FIELDS

MARK IS RUNNING through the halls of the newsroom, making his way to the production floor where they're currently live, broadcasting from the desk. He flies through, ignoring the 'On air' notifications, and makes his way to the floor producer. "Mark, what are you doing in here?" Jackie whispers aggressively.

"I have a lead."

"We're on the air!"

"I have a contact from inside Zook Towers!"

A dumbfounded look overtakes Jackie's face.

"Are you serious?"

"Yes, dead serious."

"Well, give me the info!"

"Not only do I have a contact, I have a live feed from the inside of Zook Towers."

"Give me the details and we'll get it on air."

"Hell no! So you can give it to Trent Peterson, the hack? No, this is how it's going to work. You're going to give me a cameraman and a feed. I'll deliver the exclusive and breaking news from the comm room. We need to start in three minutes!"

He turns and walks away, but Jackie calls, "Mark, wait!"

"Three minutes, Jackie! Three minutes!" he calls over his shoulder, not breaking stride.

"Shit!" Jackie exclaims. She presses her mic button, activating her headset. "Listen up, send a cameraman to meet Mark Fields in comms. We go live from that location in three minutes."

Mark throws the comms room door open at a frenzied pace and starts blurting out commands.

"Sally, I need to set up a PC with a live feed."

Sally responds, "What for?"

"Just do it!" he orders, then quickly calms down. "Okay, I'm sorry for my tone. Can you please do it? Pretty please, with sugar on top?"

"You're good to go, right there," she replies, pointing to the computer screen behind him.

"Thank you, Sally," Mark says, bringing up a browser on the computer screen. Sally walks over to take a peek at the screen. "'You bet yo' ass dot th? What kind of story are you running, here?"

Mark tilts his head slightly, saying, "Sally, please stop chomping your gum in my ear and get the hell back!"

"Okay, okay, I just want to make sure you're not pulling up a porn site or something. It's my ass on the line with this equipment."

"Sally! Will you kindly shut the f—"

Just then, the cameraman walks in.

"Good, Jason! Perfect. We're shooting right here. On me in sixty seconds!" Mark puts in his earpiece and quickly fixes his hair, wiping the sweat from his brow. "Sally, be ready to switch the channel to the computer on my signal."

The light attached to the video camera flicks on, and Jackie's voice comes over the earpiece.

"Mark, you're on in five, four, three, two…"

"Good afternoon, this is Mark Fields, coming to you live

from the broadcast room of *Channel Two News*. As most of you know, we've been following the unfolding events at Zook Towers, but like you, we've been kept in the dark as to the exact nature of this ongoing crisis. That is, until now. I have gained exclusive access to a source who claims that this is not the kind of terrorist event with which we are so sadly familiar, but rather a cover-up orchestrated by a very powerful man."

Jason pulls his face away from the camera and Sally's jaw drops so low that the gum falls out of her mouth.

"Why should we believe this?" Mark continues. "Well, this information doesn't come from the military, and it's not from our local police or the FBI. It's a gentleman by the name of Tyson Wilson who, in about ten seconds, will be broadcasting live from right inside Zook Towers." Elsewhere, every bar, household and competing news agency is locked onto their TV sets, watching Mark Fields break the story of the century. "So, any second you'll get a firsthand account of exactly what's going on inside."

All is completely silent as the camera pans over a nervous Mark Fields.

"Mark," Jackie barks in his ear, "the feed better come up in three seconds, or this will be the biggest screw-up since Geraldo Rivera opened up Al Capone's vault!"

The sweat trickles down Mark's face, just as the screen flickers on the PC. He quickly points to Sally, cuing her to make the switch.

"This is Mark Fields, giving you a first-person view of exactly what's happening." The video feed loads, and the country sees me, standing in front of the server rack.

"Hello, this is Tyson Wilson. I am broadcasting from the fiftieth floor of Zombie Towers. That's right, I said 'Zombie Towers', because this whole building is crawling with zombies. Just six hours ago, they were our coworkers, our friends. I'm joined by a few courageous survivors: Sid, who is behind the camera right now, Fickle and Vegas…" Johnny and Fickle lean in to the camera view, waving awkwardly. "We also have Matt with us…"

Matt jumps into the background and screams, "Fuck her in the pussy!"

I turn around, shocked, and shout, "Dude!" Shaking my head, I turn back to the camera. "Uh, sorry about that. So, the reason we're in this mess is because of Mr. Zook and his quest for world domination. He thought he could keep the fact that his biological weapon failed a secret, by releasing it in his own building and killing off everyone who knew about it. Well, he miscalculated, and he grossly underestimated us. Here's what's going to happen. We'll have all our cameras streaming from this website as we navigate our way out of the building, giving your viewers a firsthand perspective of what we're seeing. It serves partly for you to bear witness, but it also serves for our protection. See, we have it on good authority that Zook isn't the only one who wants this hushed up. Our military, meant to protect us as Americans, also have an interest in our silence. With the help of my good friend Sid, enjoy the show."

Sid changes the layout of the webpage from a single video stream to five separate videos, each shot by a different person's phone. Below each video is that person's name.

Safely ensconced in his estate, Fredrick J. Zook sits in his recliner, watching the broadcast about his biological weapon unfold in front of a world audience. His mood shifts from confusion to anger, from anger to terror.

After absorbing the news report, he mumbles, "This can't be happening." Throwing himself out of his chair and into the study, he screams, "*Jacobs!*"

Back in the broadcast room, Mark is once more the camera's focus.

"For those just joining, this is Mark Fields from *Channel*

Two News bringing you a live feed from inside Zook Towers or, as the hero inside put it, 'Zombie Towers'. We're going to continue to broadcast as long as possible, but be warned: due to the potentially graphic nature of what you may see, viewer discretion is advised."

The channel switches back to the video feeds, which now show the live feed from our cameras.

The light goes off on the camera, and Jason says to Mark, "Brilliant, man, this is brilliant."

Jackie speaks over his earpiece, "Wow! That was so freaking intense! Great work!"

Mark lowers the mic, pulls out his earpiece and smiles.

CHAPTER 20
TIME TO MOVE

"**A**LRIGHT MEN, EVERYONE understand the plan? We move out in five minutes," I say. I get an acknowledgment from everyone except Fick, who has his head down. "You good, Fick?"

He looks up, blinking, and says, "Hey, Tyson, can I talk to you for a sec?"

"Sure, man. What's on your mind?"

"Um, can I talk to you in private?"

At this point, none of us are really conscious of the live video streams strapped to our chests, broadcasting to *Channel Two News*. We're high on adrenaline, and our minds are elsewhere, wondering what dangers await us, and if we'll ever see freedom again. Fickle and I walk over to the far corner of the server room.

"What's up, Fick?"

"I just… I don't know if I can do it."

"Do what, man?"

"I just don't think I have what it takes to kill them… Every time I close my eyes, I see Betty and that look in her eyes. I don't think I can get past that. I feel like I might freeze up out there. I don't want to let you down, but I'm scared shitless."

Fickle hangs his head in shame.

"Hey, man," I reply. "First, there's no shame in not wanting to kill someone, but the people out there are no longer the people you know. Those people are already dead. In their place are zombies that want to chew your face off. It's kill or be killed."

"I know, I know! But—"

"Here's what's going to happen. You're going to be in charge of video surveillance. Your only job is to keep close and keep an eye on those cameras so we know what's ahead of us. You don't have to kill anyone."

A look of relief overwhelms Fick's face. He wipes his eyes and nose in an attempt to compose himself.

"You good now, man?" I ask.

"Thanks so much, Tyson. I won't let you down."

"I know you won't, man. We're in this together."

"Hey, Ty, one more thing? I'm concerned about Sid. He doesn't look very good."

I glance over at Sid; he's sweating profusely and taking short, shallow breaths.

"Yeah," I admit, "he's getting worse."

"You know, I wasn't joking," he whispers. "I watched him rape Susie in the break room. Her scarf was sucked into the shredder and he just started hammering her!"

"Geez man, that's disturbing as shit."

"What's worse, I think he has some mutated STD! I mean, look at him. He looks like he's going to die."

"Good point, man. I'll talk to him and see what's up. You'll keep your eyes on those cameras?"

"Okay, Tyson."

As Fickle walks away, I focus my attention on Sid. He looks like death, and he's starting to sound that way, too.

"Sid, can you come over here for a sec?" I ask. Sid stands up and runs over.

"What's up, Tyson?"

"You feeling okay, man?"

"To tell you the truth, I feel like shit."

"Well, you look like death! You in pain or anything?"

Sid pauses for a sec, looks back up and says, "Well, now that you mention it, I do feel like something is wrong."

"Okay, want to talk about it?"

"Well, let me show you," Sid says, unzipping his pants and pulling open his underwear to show me his crotch.

"Woah!" I gasp. "What are you doing? I don't want to see that thing!"

I really don't want to see it, but I also can't look away. It's like coming across a horrific crash with mangled bodies. You try to look away, but human nature compels you to stare. His dick is a shriveled mess; it looks like it has gangrene. It also has a slight stench, which causes me to take a step back.

"It was okay this morning, but now it looks like this."

"First, close that shit up, I'm about to vomit! Second, can you think of anything you may have done from the time you got dressed until now that may have caused that?"

"Nothing that I can think of!"

"Nothing?" I respond.

"Well, I did have sex with Susie in the break room. You think she gave me syphilis or something?"

"Dude, I'm pretty sure she gave you something, and I'm pretty sure Susie was long gone and you actually had sex with a zombie!"

"It just itches!" he says defensively, looking down at his deformed, discolored penis. He zips up his pants and walks away, leaving me to reflect that I just killed a couple of zombies in the worst way possible, and his dick is still the most repulsive thing I've ever seen.

Walking back to the group, I say, "Okay, everyone, listen up!

Just like Call of Duty but in real life, Matt's got point. Matt, that means you are in the front."

"Got it!"

"I have left flank, Vegas has right flank and Fickle is bringing up the rear as our eyes in the sky. Let's roll!"

We all line up in position, in front of the server room door. Our first goal is to get to Zook's elevator and make our way to the seventy-fourth floor, where there seems to be less zombies.

Matt slams his last beer, crushes the can on his forehead, takes a peek out of the peephole, throws the door open and says, "Time to go hunting, boys!"

*

Thailand

A skinny, rough-looking Asian fellow wakes groggily, surrounded by empty booze bottles and pizza boxes. As he sits up from the couch, a woman with severe bedhead pops up to join him. The lids of her eyes are heavy from her hangover as she slides a joint into his mouth and lights it up.

"Morning, baby!" he says mumbled by the joint between his lips. She mouths his ear as he exhales, grabs the joint from him and lays back down out of sight. Smiling, he searches the coffee table for his glasses, knocking down beer cans and chip bags in the process. He finds them, puts them on, reaches into his jean pocket and pulls out his cell phone. It takes him a moment, wiping the sleep from his eyes, to really understand the message before him, but then he jumps up, knocking the woman's head from his lap.

"What the hell?" she shouts in confusion.

"Get out!" he orders, staring at the screen.

"What?"

"I said *get the hell out!*"

She stands up, only wearing her panties, and screams, "You're an asshole!"

He ignores her frantic efforts to pick up her clothes and walks into the other room, slamming the door. She dresses quickly, throws him the finger and walks out.

"Shit, Vegas!" he mutters. "Are you serious?"

He fires up his computer, quickly types on the keyboard and pulls up youbetyoass.th There, he sees multiple camera views of Vegas and four other guys slowly walking around an office hallway, all armed with crazy weapons.

"Damn, Vegas! Is this real? Okay, okay, how can I spin this?" He thinks for a second and then looks up. "I got it!" He starts banging away at the keyboard. "This is going to be intense!" He types for a few more moments then sits back in his chair with his hands over his head. "Okay, everyone, welcome to the Z Towers survival game, where the odds are not in your favor! Betting is now live." He slowly reaches his hand over his computer mouse, slides the cursor over to 'send all', raises his index finger and slams it down on the button. Only a few seconds go by before the buy-ins start piling up. Hundreds turn to thousands, turn to tens of thousands.

"This is freaking crazy!"

CHAPTER 21

THAT WENT SOUTH FAST

A S WE WALK in close formation, Fickle remains behind, bringing up the rear.

"Looks clear around the corner, all the way to the elevator," he whispers.

"Okay," I say, "check the adjacent offices to make sure nothing surprises us." We turn the corner slowly and what do we see? A dozen zombies staring at us.

"What do we do?" Fick cries. Just then, the zombies make a run for us. Full speed. We run down the hall in the opposite direction, getting further and further from the elevator.

"What the hell, Fick? I thought you said it was all clear?"

"It was, I swear!"

"Quick, in here!" I say to the crew. We all duck into the fishbowl room. It's called 'the fishbowl' because it's a room surrounded on all sides by glass. Clearly not my best choice, but I didn't hear anyone else chime in, so here we are. Matt is the last one to come in, seeming less than thrilled to be running.

"What the hell, man?" he says, pissed off. "I thought we were here to bust some zombie skulls?"

"They caught me off guard. Now, quick, everyone down. Maybe they'll walk by."

Vegas crawls next to Fick, grabs the Surface Pro out of his hands and looks down at the screen.

"You're looking at the wrong floor, asshole!"

"What, are you sure?"

"Says it right there, you dipshit! You're looking at floor seventy! In case it's a little too hard for you, we're on floor fifty!"

"Damn guys, I'm sorry!"

"You're *sorry?* We're probably all going to die now, because of your incompetence."

"Okay, keep your voices down," I chime in, as the zombies start to meander past the fishbowl. We sit on our hands and knees, still as statues. I know we won't be able to hold this for long, and I'm not sure how thick this glass is. If needed, we can probably slip out the other side, but I need to make my way to Fickle to check the video cameras. I certainly can't trust him to do it, now. I manage to stay calm on the outside, but I'm just as pissed as Vegas. Fickle is quickly becoming a huge liability. I crawl in his direction, moving slowly enough to avoid the attention of the brain-chomping, power-suit-clad zombies outside.

"Let me see the computer," I demand. Fickle slides it over, shaking in his boots in the process.

"Fick," I say, "I need you to stay calm. This is not a time to panic."

"Okay, Tyson. I'm calm," he says shakily. I flip over the tablet and quickly switch the camera view to all cameras on the fiftieth floor. Before I can get my bearings, a brain-eating zombie bangs his head against the glass, scaring the hell out of everyone except Matt and Sid. Unfortunately, the sound grabs the attention of the zombies on the other side of the fishbowl, who are now really interested.

"Screw this!" Matt says, raising himself with his brain-splitting ax/hammer. "Time to send these spawn of Satan back to Hell!"

"Sit down and keep your voice down!" I whisper. I can tell he's all out of shits to give.

"Time to pay the piper!" he hollers, swinging the door open and bashing the first zombie so hard that blood splatters all over the hallway wall. He ducks away from an undead, swipes and swings his ax into the face of another attacker.

"Shit!" I yell, standing up to help. "Come on, guys, we need to help Matt!"

Vegas and Sid stand up and bum-rush the door to help. I look back to see Fickle frozen in the fetal position. Just as well; if he tried to help, he'd end up being zombie food in no time. As I charge them, I see that these zombies are different. They're less human; perhaps they're devolving into full-fledged brain suckers, or maybe it's my empathy that's devolving. Either way, I can still see my coworkers in them. That's Dave, right there. He always insisted on talking to me through the stalls while I was taking a dump. He used to call me his 'pooping partner'. I make my way to him and bludgeon his head, which cracks and then explodes like a watermelon. There's Madison. She had like a hundred cats and always made fur-covered brownies that she'd insist we ate. I take a full swing at her head. The sound of her skull cracking into oblivion is enough to make me sick, even without the visual of her right eye oozing out of her socket. As she crumbles in front of me, I'm overwhelmed by the nauseating smell seeping from her head. It's like someone opened a can of haggis that's been marinating in dog vomit. As I compose myself, I take a look at Matt doing his usual cowboy bullshit. It's like he was put on this earth precisely for this. He found his calling. I watch him swing his hammer so hard that it rips the top off two zombies standing next to each other. I glance at Vegas and Sid, who are tag-teaming

Randy. They haven't quite got the hang of head shots, but they're beating that poor zombie to death nonetheless. I bet it feels good; Randy always mocked Sid and was a kiss-ass to Mr. Grand. I swear I can see Sid smiling as he beats the shit out of him. I glance back at Fickle, who's watching us from inside the fishbowl. He has a look of horror on his face; I'm not sure if it's because it's a gruesome scene, or if it's because we're tearing these zombies to pieces without hesitation. Whatever the case, I turn back to the issue at hand. There's only one left, and then we'll actually have wiped these zombies out! I raise my badass bat, identifying the last attacker as Sylvia, the free-spirited girl who always smelled like flowers and talked about 'walking the earth', like in *Kung Fu*. That beautiful woman is now a zombie.

A bit of humanity slips back in for a second, and I get lost in thought about our last conversation. She and her boyfriend were planning to take this spring off, quit their jobs and walk the Appalachian Trail. She was such a sweet girl who loved everyone and everything; I often asked her about the trip, and she was so excited to share every planning detail, from the gear to the hostels they planned to stay in. I drift off in my memory of her for a moment, and I'm suddenly brought back to reality as she lunges at me. I find myself thinking that this must be how Fickle felt when he had to kill Betty; the last thing I want to do is hurt Sylvia.

I swing haphazardly, but my heart isn't in it, and I miss, burying my weapon in the wall. Sylvia isn't joking around as she continues to ravenously swipe at me, and I have to abandon my weapon to escape her grip. I reach back to find my paper cutter handle; the first weapon I used suddenly feels just right for the job. It's light and easy to maneuver, but when I look back into her eyes, I still see Sylvia and hesitate. Looking further, though, I see the gray hunger for my flesh in her eyes, the sunken sockets and rough skin, which makes me feel a little less like a monster as

I sink my cutter into her skull. Now safe, we walk back into the fishbowl and are greeted by Fickle.

"G-good job, guys. You saved my ass."

He stares at our blood-soaked faces for a good minute before vomiting all over the floor. It's then I realize that we're still broadcasting for the whole world to see. Turning my attention to the zombie at the fishbowl's other exit, I pull Vegas over and position him right in front of it, encouraging it to keep smashing its face against the window. Looking closer, I see it's Jim. He was an accountant, or something like that. He looked like a zombie even before the outbreak, so he's the perfect person to put on camera.

"What are you doing, Tyson?" Vegas asks. I wipe the blood off the front of his camera to make sure the view isn't obstructed and step in front of the viewfinder.

"Welcome to Z Towers," I announce, "where Zook has unleashed holy hell on this building and on America." I point to Jim. "This is Jim. Earlier today, Jim was drinking bad coffee and telling stupid accounting jokes. Now, he's a mindless zombie that wants to kill us. Zook is the terrorist responsible for making Jim and the countless others in this building this way, and we plan to get out of here to hold him personally accountable."

Matt perks up and walks over, saying, "Shit, I forgot we were broadcasting! Who wants to watch me bust dear old Jim's brains out the back of his head?" He gives his weapon a quick swing over his head and throws the door open. As Matt exits the fishbowl, Jim comes lunging over. Matt hits him square between the eyes with the ax side of his weapon, then spins Jim over against the fishbowl so he's clear in the view of Vegas' camera. He gives a thumbs up, Ted Nugent style, and rips out the blade, which causes Jim to wilt to the ground. Matt looks down, shoots a snot rocket and smirks. Just then, two zombies jump on his back. He screams in horror and pain, a fountain of blood spraying from his neck as one bites down.

"Holy shit!" I scream. I go to run out there and help, only to see twenty more zombies scrambling down the hallway. I quickly retreat and shut the door. Matt is already dead; there's nothing I can do to help. Vegas stands and watches in agony as Matt's face is devoured by the onslaught of zombies.

Every TV in the world is on and tuned into our youbetyoass.th footage. Suburban families, bar patrons, prisons, news agencies and Mr. Zook all watch in pure silence. The website gets updated, Matt's screen turning black. Odds are shuffled for the remaining survivors.

"*Hey!*" I call, and the zombies quickly stop chewing on Matt's lifeless body and start banging their heads and bodies on the glass to get at us.

"Let's get out of here!" Vegas yells.

"We can't!" I yell back, as the sound of teeth and skulls slamming against the glass becomes almost unbearable. "Matt has the swipe key for the elevator."

"Shit!" Vegas replies.

"Tyson!" Sid screams. "I can get it!"

"You're insane. You won't last a second out there. There's too many."

"Tyson, look at me for a sec!" I stop and look at him, but the truth is I can barely do it. He looks terrible. His eyes are graying out, and he's breathing in huge, erratic heaves. I can tell he's turning into a zombie, even if I won't admit it.

"I'm looking at you!" I say, as if it's the easiest thing in the world.

"Here's the plan. I can go out to distract them, and you guys can get the keycard off of Matt."

"That's suicide! You're way too slow. Let me go. I can run faster; I'll get them to chase me, you guys grab the key and go."

"Tyson, you're the man with the plan, the ideas. We can't risk you dying. Besides, look at me. I'm pretty sure I'm dying."

I'm about to deny it, but a trickle of blood starts to run down his nose, and his eyes are growing grayer by the second.

"I don't want to go out like this," he says, "being the first person to ever die by catching an STD from a zombie! Let me go out like a man, a hero!"

I don't even want to consider this plan, but he doesn't seem like he's going to take 'no' for an answer.

"Alright, Sid," I say begrudgingly. "What's the plan?"

"Okay, I'm going to wrap around the other side and get their attention. When you see them moving away from the windows, grab the key."

"I think this may work!" Fickle chimes in. "Looking at the Surface, it looks to be clear on that entire side."

"Okay, Sid," I sigh. "Your call."

"Okay, guys, I'm going for it!"

"Be careful, man!"

Sid walks to the door, pauses and slowly turns back.

"In the end, there's only one way out of this godforsaken building; as a mindless zombie or in a body bag. I'm choosing my fate before it chooses me. Do me a favor guys: don't tell anyone I had sex with a zombie. I don't want to be known as the guy who got an STD from a zombie."

I nod, but then look at Fick's chest, as I recall the livestream which has been broadcasting this whole time. Unfortunately, Sid notices it too. He deadpans to Fick's chest, looking right into the still-rolling camera.

"Screw it! I had sex with a zombie, and it was totally worth it!"

"Get going, you sick bastard!" I say back. Vegas and Fick walk over somberly. I think we all have the same feeling that this will be the last time we see our friend Sid.

"You be careful!" Fickle says

"Yeah man, our odds at survival are much better if you come back to us," Vegas says with a smile, patting his shoulder. Sid smiles, taking in his heroic moment. The smile slowly fades to a look of determination. He gives us a quick nod and hops over the dead zombies on the other side of the room, disappearing around the corner.

"I sure hope this works!" Vegas gripes. There are now well over twenty zombies, all trying to get at us through the glass. I can hear it starting to give way.

"We need to get out of here!" Fickle screams. "It's not going to hold."

"Just wait one sec!" I say, as we all start to back away from the glass. Just as it looks like it's going to give way, the zombies stop and turn their heads to the hallway. We can't see what's distracting them, but it has to be Sid. They all start moving away from the fishbowl.

"It's working!" I whisper. As the last one walks away, I creep to the door. Just before I open it, Matt lurches to his feet. Half of his face is gone, and blood is pouring from his neck.

"Holy shit!" exclaims Vegas. "I wasn't expecting that!"

If Matt was scary as a human, he's twice as daunting as a zombie. I kneel down so he can't see me, and he turns to follow the other zombies, quickly sprinting away.

"Well, there goes the key," I say. "Can you see Sid?"

"No, he's in a blind spot, but I can see all the zombies! Wait… he's coming back on this side, where they just were. He's fighting them off!"

We make our way back to the window and see Sid running towards the fishbowl with Matt's swipe badge in his hand and a dozen zombies on his ass.

"Come on, Sid!" I cry. "You can make it!"

Just then, he trips, and a zombie jumps on his back. He crawls under its weight, trying to reach us even as the zombie bites into his neck. He gets within ten feet of the door before he's completely swarmed by zombies and we all look away.

"No, Sid!" Vegas curses. "You almost made it, you bastard!"

We sit in silence while the zombies make their way back to the fishbowl and crowd on top of Sid. To his credit, he doesn't make a noise. This hurts. We've already lost some friends because of this bullshit, but not someone this close. Sid was our friend, and as screwed up as he was, we loved him. He risked his life to save us, and now he's gone. As we sit there feeling sorry for ourselves, not sure what fate has in store for us, I see something slip through the legs of the nearest zombie, slide under the door and come to a rest between my feet.

"It's the swipe card!" I say, and Vegas and Fickle look over at me in pure amazement. Sid did it! He saved us! He sacrificed himself so we could live. There aren't many people like that, these days. He was a true hero and a loyal friend.

"Let's take a moment to pay our respects to Sid, a true friend to the end," I say to Vegas and Fickle.

"I can't believe he did that for us," Fickle responds.

"I can't believe he had sex with a zombie!" says Vegas. Both Fickle and I turn to Vegas with shocked looks on our faces.

"What? He did!" Vegas says defensively. We can't disagree or argue the point.

We sit there for only a few seconds longer mourning our friend, Sid. He was a loyal friend until the end. You can feel the sadness overwhelming us as we take in losing him and Matt in such a short time. We can't sit here forever though. I look to my friends with a heavy heart and say, "Come on, guys! Let's get to the elevator."

CHAPTER 22
STOCKADE

THE PERIMETER AROUND the building is a complete madhouse. Thousands of people have piled against the barricades.

"Well, looks like all the freaks are out now!" Says Chief Franklin as he observes the crowd. There are people with end of the world signs, a girl in a bikini holding up an 'Eat ME!' sign and tons of others getting rowdy.

"Well, Chief," Jeffords replies, "you told him to get the media's attention."

"Yes, I did. I had no idea just how capable this guy was. Too capable."

"It looks like they're making their way to the roof."

"Good. Now, do me a favor and get the hell out of here!"

"Excuse me, Chief?"

"It's not going to take long for Sergeant Bitch-face to figure out we were the leak. When they come for us, you don't need to be here. You need to get to a spot where you can call in the helicopter. Now, get outta here!"

"Roger that, Chief. Good luck."

"Yeah, good luck to me," the chief whispers to himself as

Jeffords disappears into the crowd. "Face-eating zombies in my city and some jag-off taking control of my crime scene... I don't *feel* lucky." The chief looks over to one of the beat cops standing on the edge of the crowd and yells, "Hey, Officer!"

"Yes, Chief?"

"Come here for a sec." The officer jogs over to Chief Franklin, who glances at his badge.

"O'Malley?"

"Yes, sir!"

"You don't happen to have a smoke on you, do you?"

"Is this a trick question, sir? You know the NYPD has a strict 'no smoking on duty' policy."

"Yeah, yeah... I'm just thinking how nice it would be to have a smoke right now."

O'Malley reaches into his pocket and pulls out a box of 305s, handing a cigarette to his chief. Franklin smiles, takes it and puts it between his lips. O'Malley reaches back into his pocket and pulls out a zippo, flips it open and fires it up. The chief leans in for the light, which throws a glow on his face. As he takes a puff, he suddenly hears the sound of several automatic weapons locking on him. He lifts his head slowly and turns around to see he's surrounded by military personnel, all armed with M16s. O'Malley drops his lighter, places his hand on his side arm and steps in front of his chief.

"Stand down, Officer!" one of the soldiers yells out. O'Malley, filled with fear, replies, "Screw you, this is my chief! *You* stand down!"

Chief Franklin, cigarette still hanging out of his mouth, puts his hand on O'Malley's shoulder and says, "At ease, Officer." O'Malley takes a more relaxed posture, and the chief continues, "I'll take it from here. Go back to your post." O'Malley gives his chief a nod and starts to walk away.

"And thanks for the smoke! It will be our little secret."

"You got it, Chief," says O'Malley. He smiles, turns back and walks away. The chief redirects himself to the men who have him surrounded.

"Well, men, what's next?"

"Sir," one of the men yells. "Sergeant Major Braxton would like us to escort you to his quarters."

The chief smiles for a second and says, "Well, couldn't he have just asked?"

"We're not asking, sir. Come with us!"

"Lead the way," the chief says, smiling.

"This way, sir!"

Three men line up in front of the chief, while two men take a flank each and two guard the rear. They head over to the military comms station on the opposite side of tower two.

The chief enters a tent, held at gunpoint by three men.

"Chief Franklin!" says the sergeant major. "You have some explaining to do."

"Hello, Sergeant Major. With the hospitality I've been shown, I'm not sure I'll be explaining much."

Braxton's eyes well up in anger, and he rushes over to Chief Franklin.

"You think this is a joke? I should have you thrown in the stockade!"

"Sergeant Major, do you want to tell me what all this is about?"

"Don't play with me, Franklin! I know you and your men are behind this little show. Do you realize the risk to national security you just caused? Now, you're going to tell me about the plan you and your little monkeys inside have to get out of the building."

"With all due respect, Sergeant Major, I'm just as confused as you as to how these guys are doing what they're doing, much less how they plan to get out."

"Bullshit! We know you talked to him. Now, I'm going to ask one last time. Tell me what you know. I'm trying to save the lives of thousands of people here, Chief! If you don't tell me, I have the authority to lock you up for two years without due process. Did you know that?"

"I understand your capabilities perfectly clearly," the chief replies grimly. "A biological agent got into my city somehow, after all, and without this 'little show', it seems like you'd have already covered up the fallout, even if it meant killing a few Americans. All in the name of national security, right? No disrespect, Sergeant Major, but you can kiss my big, black, *New York* ass!"

"Get him out of here!" Braxton booms, and two MPs slip their hands under the chief's armpits. He pushes them off.

"Get your hands off me, I can walk!"

He walks out of the tent with the MPs trailing close behind.

CHAPTER 23
WHAT NOW?

FICK, VEGAS AND I scramble to Zook's elevator. It's clear right now, but we know zombies are right around the corner. I quickly wipe the ID card off on my pants, clearing off the blood, and swipe it. Breathing deep, I punch a button.

"It lit up," I murmur, and we all stand there staring at this little, illuminated button. Now, all we have to do is survive the time it takes for the elevator to arrive. Fick is clearly uncomfortable.

"Hurry up, hurry up, hurry up!" he whispers, like a three-year-old that has to pee.

"Shh, Fick," I reply. I'm not sure how much time passes before the doors open. It might be ten seconds or it might be ten minutes. *Ding!* We pile in and the door closes behind us as we collectively exhale a long sigh of relief. A little less tense, we take a few seconds to relax behind the safety of the closed elevator doors.

"Okay, let's stay with the plan," I say. "Fick, how does it look on Zoe's floor?"

Fick stands in silence for a second, then says, "Oh man, I left the Surface in the fishbowl!"

"*What?* Dammit Fick, you're killing me! You had one job,

and you couldn't even do that right! We lost Matt and Sid because of you! You're useless."

I know being hard on Fick isn't particularly helpful, but in the moment, I can't help it.

"I'm going to fix it!" Fick says as he punches the 'open door' button on the elevator. The door opens, and he spots the waiting zombies, led by Matt and Sid. They turn slowly as he begins stabbing at the 'close door' button.

"Come on, come on!" he whines as the door closes.

"Well, you almost got us killed again," I snipe. "You're batting a thousand here, Fick! Any more great ideas?"

"Hey, let's all calm down" Vegas chimes in.

"What do we do now?" Fick asks.

"Okay, okay, let me think," I say, pausing like I'm on the brink of a fabulous idea. Really, I have no idea what to do. Without eyes in the sky, we have no idea what we'll be running into when the doors open. Frankly, without Matt and Sid, we're totally screwed! Suddenly, the elevator starts to move up.

"It's moving!" Vegas cries. "You think it's Zook?"

"Not many people have access to his elevator," Fickle replies.

"No way it's Zook," I reply. "That asshole is *long* gone. Be prepared for anything!"

Vegas and I get into an offensive stance, with our weapons raised high. Fick doesn't have shit; I'd put good money on him not surviving much longer. Hell, *I* may kill him before we get off this elevator.

The elevator continues its way up… 70, 71, 72, 73, 74, 75! Ground zero of the outbreak. Oh, we're screwed for sure.

"No, not here," Fick says.

"Be ready!" I whisper, but as the door opens, we're greeted by a shotgun barrel. I throw my hands up, and only then do I see it's Zoe. She sees it's us and smiles.

"We have to stop meeting like this," she says. I'm overwhelmed with excitement when I see her, and we gaze into each other's eyes as I step out of the elevator. She lowers her gun, inviting me in closer, and I step in, wetting my lips, closing my eyes and leaning in for a kiss.

"Woah, woah!" she exclaims as she pushes me back. "We aren't there yet, Tyson! Now, why in the hell do you all have cell phones strapped to your chests?"

"Dammit!" I say out loud, realizing that the entire world just saw me getting rejected. "Everyone, pause your video." I look over to Zoe and explain, "We're livestreaming to show the whole world what's happening here."

"Well, you don't know the half of it. I'm pretty confident that Zook was losing his contract with the military and he had his pet, Jacobs, purposely unleash a biological weapon in the building."

"I knew it!" I crow. "And I always knew that scumbag was evil! We're going to blow the lid off his fake-ass empire."

"Well, what now, boys?"

"Zook's penthouse!" I say excitedly. I step back in the elevator and hold the door open for Zoe.

"Milady," I say as she steps in.

"You're such a gentleman."

Jeffords makes his way into a local bar, where he sees everyone is crowding around the TVs. He bellies up and leans in to the bartender.

"Whiskey."

"Whiskey, coming up."

Jeffords pulls out his phone and places it next to him on the bar. The bartender slides down a shot glass full of whiskey, and Jeffords reaches out his hand, grabs it and slams it back.

"Keep 'em coming," he says, and the bartender nods. Jeffords sits on the bar stool, angling himself to get a clear view of the TV. The people in the bar are captivated by the livestream. For a bar that's usually loud and boisterous, you could hear a pin drop right now.

"Pretty screwed up!" the bartender says, as he slides over another whiskey.

"You have no idea," Jeffords responds, slamming back another shot.

The elevator door opens on the penthouse suite, and we step out. Zoe takes the lead; man, she is even hotter handling that gun! We move into different rooms, making quick work of checking for zombies.

"Clear!" Zoe says from one of the rooms.

"Clear," says Vegas from the opposite side.

"All clear here," I say, walking into the kitchen area. Man, Zook lived large, up here. This place is a mansion!

"I have a locked door!" Fickle exclaims. Zoe quickly walks over, telling Fick to stand back, and kicks the door open. Throwing up her shotgun, she walks in.

"All clear!"

All astonished, we slowly follow her in. We're now standing in Zook's security room and holy shit, we thought our server room was decked! There must be fifty monitors here.

"Hey, guys," Fickle calls out. "There are people down there. Survivors!" Sure enough, as we walk up to take a closer look at the screens, you can see a couple of people hiding, fighting or just running for their lives in the building below.

"We have to help them!" Fick says.

"We can't help them," I respond. "We can barely help ourselves!"

"Yeah, it's suicide!" Vegas agrees. "It's a miracle we even made it up here."

"We can't leave them behind!"

"Listen to me, Fick," I say calmly. "We can't help them; we're almost out of here, almost safe."

"You're so full of shit, Tyson!" Fickle howls, his voice cracking. "You fed us this line about humanity and how saving Zoe was important because she was a person, but it turns out you just wanted to get in her pants!"

"Hey man, I never said that!" I turn to look at Zoe. "I never said that."

She looks over to Fick and says, "He's right."

"Wait, not you too!" I reply.

"If we leave people behind, we're no better than Zook and his little weasel, Jacobs! If we turn our backs on these people, on their families, we'll never be able to live with ourselves."

Shit, now Fick has Zoe all fired up for the greater good!

"Okay, okay, I'm in," I say reluctantly. "But we're going to do this my way!" I look over to Vegas, who nods in agreement. "First, though, I need to do something. Fick, come over here." Fickle walks over slowly, almost as if he's going to get in trouble.

"Hey, Tyson, sorry, I just think it's the—"

"Shut up, Fick. You're right, I'm wrong. We need to save as many people as possible. Now, stand up straight!"

Fick does as I ask, and I hit 'record' on the camera still taped to his shirt.

"Hello, ladies and gentlemen. As you can see, we've been dealing with some pretty screwed-up shit thanks to the great Fredrick J. Zook and his asshole-kissing buddy, Jeremy Jacobs. Turns out Zook has been working with our star-spangled military to create a biological weapon that's capable of decimating entire continents by turning them into brainless zombies. He's created this weapon right here, in the good ol' USA's backyard, and when life didn't go his way, he unleashed it onto his own people. To shut them up, to show them his power, to prove he always gets his way, like a child throwing a temper tantrum, he took his ball and went home, leaving us here to die! So, I'm here to tell the entire world, right now, that there is a real terrorist amongst us, and he's one of us, an American. His name is Fredrick J. Zook, and he's responsible for the deaths of thousands of Americans. Now, we're working our asses off to save as many as we can, but we need more time. So, those who are supposed to be listening, give us more time, and pray for us. We've already lost so much. God bless you, and god bless the United States of America."

CHAPTER 24
FIGURING IT OUT

ZOOK WATCHES AS the stream that has just exposed him fades to darkness. He slowly puts his hands over his face, leans back and takes a deep breath.

"Sir," says Jacobs, approaching his boss, "we need to stay focused. Our plan is in motion. Americans will be forever in your debt, for your patriotism."

"Oh, shut up, Jacobs!" Zook squeals. "Did you just watch what I watched? We're done for! And how did he get access to my penthouse?"

"Sir, stay the course. You know the protocol. There's no way anyone leaves that building alive."

"They don't *have* to leave! They're broadcasting live for the whole damn world to see. How the hell are they doing *that*, Jacobs? All communication is supposed to be cut off!"

"I don't know, sir. I've confirmed that all traffic in and out of the building is down. They must have found an alternate route."

"Yes, but *how*, you moron?"

"I don't know, sir, but you do always hire the best and brightest. Obviously, they figured it out."

"'Best and brightest'? Go screw yours... Wait! A couple of

months ago, I signed a purchase order for an alternate secure fiber connection because I thought the government was wiretapping me. I also requested it not be listed in the schematics, so no one would know it existed. Get whoever is in charge at ground zero on the phone. We may be able to spin this, yet. Let's make it all that little jerk-offs fault. What was his name?"

"Tyson, sir."

"Well, 'Tyson', you're going to learn not to screw with Zook. Come on, Jacobs. Make some calls!"

"Yes, sir!"

From a stool in the local bar, Jeffords watches as the feed fades to black. The entire bar is eerily quiet, and everyone seems deeply disturbed by the events unfolding. An enormous, rough-looking biker with long hair and a grizzled beard stands and speaks in a deep voice.

"Screw Zook! That asshole is a terrorist! I say we all march the hell down there and bust some zombie skulls!"

The bar remains quiet for a few seconds, until a squirrelly, nerdy guy slowly rises to his feet and walks up to the biker, who is double his size. He holds out his hand, and the biker shakes it.

As he and the biker lock hands, the squirrelly guy hollers, "You don't screw with New Yorkers! Come on, everyone, let's go!"

The entire bar erupts in anger and marches out the door towards Zook Towers.

As the bar empties, Jeffords remains on his stool. He pulls out his phone and starts typing a text. It reads, 'Helicopter extraction delayed for now, stay tuned'. He hits send, looks down at his empty shot glass, looks over to the bartender and raises an eyebrow. The bartender nods, walks over with a bottle of whiskey and tops off the glass.

"How come you're not running out with the mob?" he asks.

Looking deep into his glass, Jeffords responds, "I'm better served right here. You just keep that TV on and the refills coming."

"Roger that," responds the bartender.

From the comm center at ground zero, Braxton watches as I blame the military and Zook for the zombie outbreak inside Zook Towers. As the video fades to black, he looks around, frustrated. He walks over to a table covered with building schematics and comm equipment, and in a burst of anger, clears it off with a single swipe of his hand.

"Can anyone in here tell me how the hell, with all this equipment, all this intel, this guy is still broadcasting for all to see?"

Everyone pauses to look up, but it's clear that no one has any answers.

"Let's go, people!" Braxton bellows. "I need to know how we can shut down his feed!" He stops for a second, recalling Tyson's exact words. "It was a code! He's buying time." He rushes over to an MP. "Go get Chief Franklin and bring him to my tent."

"Yes, sir!"

As Braxton and the MP go to leave, a member of the comms team yells out, "Excuse me, Sergeant Major?"

"What?"

"I have a Jeremy Jacobs on the line, he says he's calling on behalf of Mr. Fredrick Zook."

Braxton stares for a moment before responding, "Send the comm to my tent!"

"Yes, sir."

CHAPTER 25

SAVING LIVES,
KILLING ZOMBIES

"**O**KAY, EVERYONE, CIRCLE up in the security room."
I'm suddenly enraged, after my speech. Just the thought that Zook and people like him have such disregard for everyday people pisses me off. He puts himself above everyone else, and it makes me sick. He threw us away like trash! I need to focus; I can't let emotion overwhelm me now. We already lost Sid and Matt, and I'm not losing anyone else.

"Okay, guys, here's the plan. First thing we need to do is go for some easy wins." I scan the monitors looking for some movement on the closer floors. "There!" I cry, pointing to three people barricaded in an office suite with five zombies outside their door. "What floor is that?"

"It's floor seventy," Zoe responds.

"Okay. Fick, you stay here. Vegas, Zoe and I will—"

"Hell no, I'm not staying here!" Fickle says matter-of-factly.

"Fick, you don't have it in you, man," I reply. "You're a liability out there, and I'm not sure we can protect you. The best play is for you to—"

"Screw that, Tyson. You're not my mother! I know I haven't exactly contributed so far, but seeing these people locked down and scared, I want to be there for them. I'm going!"

"Okay," I say, shrugging. I can't exactly ban him when he persuaded me to go in the first place. "Well, I guess we're all going. We need to stick together, anyway."

Zoe chimes in, "I'm going to the lobby!"

"Umm, hell no..." I respond. She cocks her shotgun. "Well, we can talk about it," I say nervously. "Let's talk about it!"

"See there?" she says, pointing to the screen that shows security guards locked in a room. "Those are my friends, my coworkers. They're locked in there, waiting to die, because they know the protocol is to do just that. But they don't know what I know; that this breach, this infection, was intentional. I need to go get them. Plus, they'll be able to help us; they're trained for this!"

"This plan still sucks," I protest. "We only have one elevator. What happens if you need it and we're using it? Ever think about that?"

"*You* think too much," she says with a smile. "We all get in together, I drop you guys off on floor seventy and take it down to the lobby. When I get off, I'll send it up to you and make my way to the security room. I'll hang out there for ten minutes and call it back. We both have ID cards for the elevator, so we're good. Just don't dilly dally."

"There are a lot of variables that could go wrong here," I reply. "It's not that simple. Take a look at the lobby; there are hundreds of zombies down there. It's a suicide mission."

"I can handle myself! Besides, I'm not asking. Let's go!" she calls as she walks over to the elevator.

"What you're describing is exactly what goes wrong in every damn zombie movie ever written," I shout. "The last thing we should do at this point is separate. If you're going to the lobby, we're all going to the lobby!"

"I'm in," Fick says.

"Screw it!" Vegas chimes in.

I walk up to Zoe and gently lower the tip of her shotgun.

"We do this together," I say, leaning in, and she nods in agreement. Vegas and I walk up to Zoe's bag of weapons, while Zoe waits by the elevator and Fick continues to study the video feeds. We each grab a couple of handguns and preloaded magazines, and start shoving them into our waistlines. Having guns will be a lot more effective than swinging the paper cutter, but to be honest, I've grown to love the thing, so I tuck it into my belt strap. I notice that Vegas grabbed his table leg, too. Guns are efficient, but there's something about defending yourself with something you can swing. We make our way to Zoe, who is holding the elevator open, allowing us to load in, and we're off to the lobby.

I'm not feeling good about this. Zoe is a badass, and we're better armed than we were before, but we certainly aren't trained to handle these situations like she is, ammo or not. But hey, at least we have guns... Well, except Fickle. He doesn't have anything. I guess he's going to kill zombies with his personality. Idiot! This plan sucks!

The elevator ride seems to last forever, as we all stand silently watching the numbers count down. I suddenly feel very ill, trying to ready myself for whatever we're about to encounter on the bottom floor. As the elevator slows, I quickly reach over and hold the 'close door' button, my heart beating a thousand miles a minute. I've grown accustomed to the blood and death, but after losing Sid, I'm overwhelmed by the fear of losing anyone else. I don't think I could take it if anyone died, even Fickle.

"Hey, guys," I murmur, "do we just go in guns blazing, or do we have a plan?"

Zoe says, "You guys ever play first-person shooter games, like *Call of Duty*?"

"Hell yeah, you're looking at the 'Bazinga Clan', the highest ranked and most sought-after clan in *COD*!" I realize just how nerdy I sound and try to regroup. "I mean, it's a pretty prestigious ranking in the gaming community, but we don't take it seriously."

"Impressive!" Zoe says. "I'm on the 'NY Killer' squad."

"What? We've had some epic battles with that clan!"

Man, not only is this girl a badass in real life, but she's also a gamer! I'm not sure she can get any better. I'm in love!

"Listen," she says, "it's easy. Just like *COD*; we're going to do a compressed squad column. Stay in tight formation, about three feet apart. I'll take point. Vegas, you're on my left flank. Ty, you're on my right. Fick, you bring up the rear!" Zoe reaches behind her back, pulls out a 9mm and hands it to Fickle. His eyes light up like an excited (but scared) little boy.

"Everyone hold their positions," she continues. "Stay on my point, and for the love of god, don't get trigger happy! Use your bullets wisely, and aim for the head. Anyone have any questions?"

"Will you marry me?" I blurt out. She smiles, hits the 'open door' button and gets in position.

"Gut up, boys! This is going to get a little hairy."

The doors open and we step out in unison, like a professional kill squad. The lobby is crawling with zombies, but at this point, they're dormant. They stumble around aimlessly, bouncing off the walls and furniture.

"No one make a sound," Zoe whispers as we slowly make our way to the security room. We nod, quietly but efficiently gliding across the lobby floor. It's located in almost a straight line from where we entered, but it's about a football field away. If we can make it without being seen, things will turn out much better than the scenario that played out in my head on the elevator ride down. Fick is holding his gun close to his chest, but when he looks down, he notices he's not livestreaming. He reaches down, struggling to turn on his camera, and drops his gun in the process. We all stop dead as the sound of metal hitting a marble floor ripples through the otherwise silent lobby. I look over at Fickle in utter disdain and then swivel back to my flank position. I eyeball Zoe, who has her shotgun at point and is still as a rock. After what seems to be forever, it looks like we're in the clear. Some of the zombies pause for a second, but the lobby's size means they only heard a distorted echo, and they don't know where to look. Soon, they're back to shuffling aimlessly around the lobby.

We start to back up slowly, and I glance back to see Fickle breathe a sigh of relief and reach down to get his gun. His fingers close around it, and as he picks it up, he inadvertently fires off a shot! The sound is deafening. We freeze again, hoping for a lucky break, but the echo is flatter, and every zombie spins in our direction. There's a beat, and then they're rushing towards us. There are probably a hundred of them, maybe more.

"Move!" Zoe exclaims, beginning to shoot off one careful shot after another "Head shots only!"

Vegas and I follow suit, targeting only the most immediate threats to our flanked zones, watching the blood splatter after each careful shot. Fick brings up the rear, spraying bullets all over the place like a madman. Not only is he not getting head shots, I'm pretty sure he's not hitting anything. And just like that, he's out of bullets, although he continues to rapid fire like he's actually doing something. Useless!

"Holy shit, look!" says Frank, pointing to the main lobby camera. "There's a group with guns making their way through the lobby!"

Derek runs over to look, then says, "That's Zoe!" He pauses for a second. "Quick guys, weapons hot! Dylan, open the door. Let's get out there and get our soldier."

Frank, Dylan and Derek get into position at the door with weapons drawn. Dylan throws the doors open and they rush out.

"Reloading!" I scream as the hoard of zombies, tripping their way over the dead, make their way closer to our squad. I drop my clips, pull two new ones out of my waistband and reload in short order. I'm amazed just how awesome we are at this. I have some experience with guns, as Vegas and I have spent some time hanging out at the shooting range on the weekends. But man, I feel like John McClane in *Die Hard*, right now. Although we're kicking ass, I'm also realistic; I see the writing is on the wall. This will be the place we all die. The bullet-to-zombie ratio just isn't in our favor. I share a glance with Vegas, who's reloading his own gun. Everything is in slow motion. I can tell by the look in his eyes that he's calculated the odds and knows it's only a matter of minutes until we succumb to the worst death imaginable: being eaten to death or, worse, getting bitten and becoming one of them. I stop shooting for a second and contemplate putting a bullet in my own head, instead. I have plenty of fight left in me, but I know what reality holds for me. At least I'll go on my own terms and not have to feel the agony of being torn apart by these monsters. Still, I have my friends, and I need to do whatever it takes to protect them. *Not now*, I think to myself, ejecting a bullet from the chamber to grab it in mid-air like they do in the movies. Unfortunately, I miss, and the bullet actually bounces off my left eye. I take three swipes at it before it clinks to the ground, then bend down to pick it up. I want to make sure I have one left, in case it comes to that, but for now, I need to help my friends.

"This way!" calls a voice from out of the darkness of approaching zombies. Suddenly, rapid fire is coming from a different direction. Light starts to appear, as we watch the heads of zombies explode right in front of us.

Zoe yells, "It's Derek! Everyone, on me! Go, go, *go!*"

We tighten up our formation, and the light of the security doors leads the way. We're now completely covered in blood, brains and who knows what else. Fick is completely on my back at this point, as he has nothing to protect himself. We hastily make our way to the security room, as a barrage of bullets slings past our ears. Making it to the security doors is sincerely surreal. We lunge our way in, and two of the security guards slam the door behind them.

"Damn, Zoe!" says Derek. "You're one crazy woman!"

Zoe stands up with a slight grin on her face.

"Well, someone had to come save your sorry asses," she says, and they share a smile that makes me think they're more than just friends.

"Hey there, buddy," I say, standing quickly. "Thanks for the crossfire. Name's Tyson!"

Derek reaches out his hand, saying, "Hey there, Tyson, my name's Derek, this is Dylan and Frank."

I nod to each guy, giving my best man-squeeze on Derek's hand. He doesn't seem impressed, so I pull away. Derek is a tall, physically fit dude, with short blonde hair and blue eyes. I'm sure he gets a lot of ladies with his tough-guy swagger. Dylan also looks pretty fit; he could be Derek's brother, for all I know. These aren't the type of genes I've been blessed with. Frank, on the other hand, looks like he's been here a while. He's short and chubby, with a receding hairline and a mustache.

"This is Fickle and Vegas," I say, "and of course you know Zoe."

"*Know* her? Zoe and I go way, way back!"

I suddenly hate Derek.

"Really, that's interesting. So, how far back? Like, high school sweethearts? Zoe, is this your boyfriend?"

With an innocent smile, Zoe looks over to me and says, "Derek and I went through boot camp together."

"Oh, yes! We sure did," Derek says with a wink.

"What's that supposed to mean?" I say in an agitated voice.

"It means nothing," Zoe quips back. "Derek likes to screw

with guys that seem interested in me. He's like a father more than a boyfriend. He's harmless, and no threat to you."

"Oh, okay. Well, in that case, can I call you 'Dad'?"

As I reach out to shake Derek's hand again, he smirks but doesn't seem too happy about my comment. That's okay by me. The only thing worse than a beautiful woman who puts you in the friend zone is one who throws you into the dad zone. Ouch! Instead of laying it on too thick, I decide I should show a bit of gratitude to these guys. I have no doubt that we'd be dead right now if they hadn't come out guns blazing.

"Seriously, guys, you saved us big time," I say. "We were toast out there; we'd be goners if it wasn't for you."

Derek nods in appreciation and makes his way to Zoe.

"Zoe, what's the deal? You know protocol. In the case of a level one lockdown, we're supposed to hold our posts."

"I know, Derek, but this didn't happen by accident. Zook and Jacobs intentionally unleashed the biohazard to wipe out everyone in this building."

"What? How... *Why?*"

"We're still putting that together, but I believe he didn't hear what he wanted to hear when the Pentagon visited him today, and he wanted to take out the people who knew about his agent."

"That sounds crazy, even for someone as unstable as Zook!"

"I know, but I saw it with my own eyes. Jacobs orchestrated the release before getting on the elevator and leaving the building! We need to get out of here before they come in and napalm this whole building. He can't get away with this, Derek!"

Derek paces around the room, trying to make sense of it all while also struggling with following protocol.

After a minute or two he says, "Okay, what's the plan?"

"I thought you'd never ask!" I say with a smile. I turn to Fickle and point to his chest. "Fick, turn off the feed!" Fickle looks down and shuts off the feed, which I'm not even sure is working anymore. I turn my attention back to Derek, saying, "I'm working with someone on the outside that will provide us with a helicopter ride off the roof. All we need to do is get our happy asses to the penthouse and wait for our ride."

"Just like that?"

"Yep, just like that."

"Zoe," says Derek, "you know we aren't supposed to leave. Now, I hear where you're coming from on Zook. I've never trusted that self-serving, sick-old-pedophile-looking, stubby-toed, money-grubbing asshole, but protocol is protocol."

"I know, Derek! You're a great soldier, but that's *Zook's* protocol you're following. He's no soldier, he's never served; he was born into money and telling people what to do. Bottom line, he has no honor. You do!"

Derek contemplates this for a while, sizing us up and sharing a few glances with his two boys. At this point, I'm not really sure this trip to the lobby was worth it.

"Okay, we're in!" Derek exclaims. He turns and walks slowly in Zoe's direction. "If what you say is true, Zoe, Zook needs to go down hard for this."

I jump up and rush to Zoe's side, putting my arm around her and saying, "Well, alright, cowboy. Let's get the hell out of here!"

Zoe smiles slightly at my attempt at affection. It builds up my confidence, so I try to take my assertiveness to a new level.

"Okay, here's the plan! First thing we nee—"

My voice is suddenly drowned out by the sound of guns being loaded and cocked.

I look over to Derek, who says, "We got it from here, 'cowboy'. You just stay on our six."

I have to be honest; I haven't felt this secure since running the zombie gauntlet with Matt, although Matt was more entertaining. These guys are pros; we may get out of here yet!

CHAPTER 26
FALLING INTO PLACE

BRAXTON IS BACK in his tent, just hanging up the phone, when the MP brings in Chief Franklin.

"Well, hello Chief!" Braxton says with an air of confidence.

"Hello, Sergeant Major. Quite the crowd you have building out there."

Braxton looks over to the huge crowd of people amassing outside the perimeter. The crowd is made up of all types of people, from construction workers to soccer moms, all trying to get a glimpse of what's happening at Zook Towers.

"Yeah, seems like someone has them all riled up. Someone by the name of 'Tyson'. Ever heard of him?"

"Can't say that I have."

As Franklin walks deeper into the tent, the MP excuses himself.

"Interesting," says Braxton, taking a few steps closer to the chief. "Well, I just got off the phone with the one and only Fredrick J. Zook. He tells me he has it on good authority that this Tyson fellow is a domestic terrorist who intentionally released a biological weapon in the building, causing this whole mess."

"And I bet you're just dumb enough to believe him."

"You tell me, Chief! I mean, Zook is respected by our military; many consider him a patriot. Meanwhile, this Tyson fellow is streaming video of him and his cohort of thugs running around the building, hacking up zombies and trying to pin it all on Zook."

The chief stands up straight, takes a deep breath and says, "Why am I here, Sergeant Major?"

"I'm hoping you can help me. There are a lot of bystanders here. We don't want anyone else to get hurt. Tell me what you know, and we can work together to save lives."

"Sorry, Sergeant Major, can't help you. I wish I could."

"Well then you, Chief, will be solely responsible for the deaths of more innocent citizens. If anyone breaches the quarantine area, I have the authority to napalm a three-block radius. Look outside, Chief!"

The chief slowly turns his head to see the mob of New Yorkers congregating around the area.

"Now," says Braxton, "you don't want to see any of those people hurt, I know you don't. Tell me what you know. Let's work together to end this!"

The chief's shoulders slump in despair. The entire weight of the city's safety now rests squarely upon them. He sighs and thinks for a moment.

"I'm not going to trade one American's life for another," he says, standing resolute. "This is New York City. We have each other's backs here! You want to send me to prison, go ahead and take your chances, but I will be damned if I'm going to let you murder innocent Americans in the name of security! You, Sergeant Major, can go to hell!"

Braxton strides over with a scowl, drawing himself up into the chief's face.

"Have it your way, Chief! The blood will be on your hands!"

The two stand toe-to-toe in a deadlock stare, neither giving in to the other's intimidation tactics. Eventually, Braxton whistles, and an MP walks in.

"Take Chief Franklin back to his tent. He won't be going anywhere for a long, long time."

Zook hangs up the phone, pulls a new cigar from his gold-plated humidor and lights it up. He reaches down to his glass of scotch, swirls the ice around, pulls out the cigar, blows out a puff and then takes a swig.

"Jacobs! Get your ass in here!"

Jacobs walks in with his hands behind his back.

"Yes, sir," he says subordinately.

"We have a new plan. I've convinced our guy on the ground that Tyson is behind this whole thing. We need to drum up some evidence that points to him."

"Yes, sir" Jacobs replies, turning to walk out of the room.

"Wait, I'm not done yet!"

"Sir?"

"We're going to have to call off the sale, too."

"Sir, I think that's a mistake. We're so close!"

"Jacobs, I know you put a lot of effort in here, and you'll be rewarded, but this is the only play, right now. All eyes are on me, and I need to clean up this mess."

"Sir, I strongly suggest you reconsider."

"Hey, you don't call the shots here, I do! Now, I said 'cancel the sale'. You work for me, boy!"

Jacobs pauses for a moment to take in what Zook is telling him, then says, "I'm afraid I can't let you do that, sir."

"You don't tell me what to do, got it? Jacobs, I love you, but I'll cut your throat and send you down the river if I have to."

Jacobs pulls out a silenced 9mm handgun and points it directly at Zook.

"Whoa, whoa, calm down! Put that damn gun away!"

"You forced my hand, sir."

"Okay, let's talk!" Zook says shakily.

"Wow!" Jacobs says, full of confidence. "I always knew you were a coward, but I didn't think you'd fall apart so quickly. I already see the fear in your eyes and... are you about to cry? I mean, I point a gun in your direction, and you practically piss you pants. I figured you would at least fake it for a bit!"

"Now, calm down, Jacobs. We can still make the sale. And you can get your cut."

"Oh, I don't care about your money. Do you honestly think I'm motivated by this sale?"

"Then, what... what do you want?" Zook responds, quivering.

"This was never about money, for me. It's about rebooting this world, this sick damn world and the human race. I was hoping that, through your greed, you would start the apocalypse. I thought maybe you would have the balls to pull it off, but I didn't have that much faith, so I do have my own plan B, and that's Genesis. It's time to end the suffering and start anew. Unfortunately, my plan B doesn't end well for you, Zook."

"Jacobs, please! After all I've done for you!"

"For me, you self-serving asshole? You've been nothing but rotten. You're part of the problem; the reason I'm doing this. You and your greed, you cause nothing but destruction and mayhem."

With his gun still trained on Zook's head, Jacobs slowly walks towards him. Sobbing uncontrollably, Zook collapses in fear.

"Have you no balls at all?" Jacobs spits, looming over him. "All that tough talk, and here you are begging little ol' me to spare your life. Don't worry, I'm not going to kill you."

"Y-you're not?"

"No, plan B is so much better than that!"

CHAPTER 27
MOVING ON UP

"**A**LRIGHT, EVERYONE, HERE'S the plan!" Derek says in the security control room. "I'll take point. Zoe, Dylan, you take flank right and left. Frank, you take up the rear. You three..." He points to me, Fickle and Vegas. "...stay in the center and move when we move."

"Wait, we don't need you to protect us! We've done just fine without you, and we've been out there, kicking ass and taking names."

"Come on, Tyson," Fickle chimes in. "I think this is a good plan!"

"Of course you do; you don't have a chance to screw it up!"

"This plan is non-negotiable," Derek says authoritatively.

"Well, I think your plan sucks!"

To be honest, it's a fine plan, but it's the second time in a row that an executive decision has been made without me. I don't like others determining my fate, and I especially don't like it from this GI Joe.

"We gonna have a problem, son?" Derek snaps back.

"Son?" I say, taking exception. "I know you're old as dirt, but you're not my daddy, and I don't take orders from you!"

Zoe walks over, puts her hand on my shoulder and says, "Listen, Tyson. I know you can handle yourself. These guys are very tactical, whereas you're more of a raw badass. Let them do their thing. I need you to cover my six!"

Suddenly feeling better, I give Zoe a quick wink and then look past her, to where Derek is standing in his 'Captain Morgan' pose.

"Alright, Derek, you're the boss," I say. "Let's do this!"

"Okay, our target is Zook's private elevator, which will get us to the penthouse suit. Tyson, you want a job? Take the swipe card and open those elevator doors. We'll hold off the zombies until we're clear."

"Mission accepted, Your Holiness," I say, holding up the swipe card. Derek clearly doesn't like my tone, but he proceeds with the plan.

"Everyone in position," he orders, and we arrange ourselves in a 'V' formation, like a flock of birds. Derek holds up his hand, holds up three fingers, then two, then one and finally a solid fist. He throws the doors open and we are instantly met with what seems like hundreds of zombies. The barrage of gunfire is deafening. We slowly make our way out to the lobby. Fick, Vegas and I can't see anything but the backs of our own security detail.

"Reloading!" Derek screams, and he and Dylan rotate positions to give him the time he needs. I have to admit, these guys are moving like a synchronized swimming team. As we make it to the halfway point, I'm feeling pretty good. I glance over to Zoe, who is impressively administering head shot after head shot. Me and this girl are going to make some fantastic babies together. I can see us at the playground, me pushing our daughter on the swing while she sits on the bench, breastfeeding our son. We blow kisses and make goofy faces at each other. I'm suddenly in complete bliss.

"I'm *jammed!*" Frank yells out from the back. I snap out of my daydream and turn to see Frank get overwhelmed by zombies.

"Hey, Frank's down!" I scream at Derek. He turns quickly and assesses Frank, who is now screaming as zombies chew away his flesh.

"Sorry, Frank!" Derek yells, and then turns his gun and shoots Frank in the head. "Tyson, you take the rear!"

Shit! He snuffed out his friend, just like that. I get it: Frank was as good as dead, but Derek didn't flinch. I wish I could have done that for Sid. I feel so terrible, knowing how he went out while I laid helpless. Sid deserved better. I find myself respecting Derek just a little. There was a lot of honor in that kill.

"I'm on it," I shout, pulling two handguns from my waistband and firing into the zombie crowd. It's amazing how calm I am. The blood and brain splatter does nothing to phase me at this point. Just hours before this, I would have buried my face in a pillow with shit like this. Now, I'm doing what I need for survival. I'm grateful for such a quick evolution, but terrified at the thought of never being normal again. I need to get out of my head and just focus on the job at hand; I can question my humanity, or what's left of it, after this is over. For now, I need to focus on surviving.

"Tyson! You're up, swipe us in!"

Just like that, we're at the elevator. Only one casualty to get here, and my boys are still intact. Derek, Zoe and Dylan pivot, facing away from the elevator, holding off the horde. I swipe the card and the doors open. We all back in, firing until the doors close. Only then do we take a breath, and I tap Derek on the shoulder.

"Hey, man, I know that was hard. We've lost two, so far. Frank died a hero!"

Derek nods in appreciation, hits the top floor button and up we go.

We stand quietly in the elevator, watching each floor go by. The silence is necessary. I know Derek and Dylan are going through some shit in their heads, right now. They seem like a tight group, and the loss of Frank is probably hitting them pretty hard. Suddenly, Fickle starts yammering.

"Wait! We need to stop on the seventieth! There are survivors there!"

Derek responds, "That's not our mission, right now."

"Hey, I get it, you lost your friend. That sucks!" Fickle says. "But we risked our lives to save you, and we plan on saving more!" Fickle reaches out to hit the seventieth-floor button, but Derek smacks his hand away.

"I told you, boy, that's not our mission!"

"Hey!" I say, feeling the need to defend Fick. "Back the hell off! This guy, right here, doesn't want to kill anyone, he only wants to save people. Show a little respect!"

Derek looks straight ahead, makes no eye contact and says, "The mission is to get to the penthouse. We can assess from there."

"That's *your* mission," I reply. "Ours is to stop by the seventieth floor to help more people." I quickly press the seventieth-floor button, much to the delight of Fick, but not Derek. If looks could kill, his stare would have killed me three times already. "Listen," I say, "we need to do this. No one is asking you to help. Fick, Vegas and I will check out the seventieth for survivors. You guys go up to the penthouse to recon or whatever it is that you plan to do up there."

"Do what you want!" Derek says, still not making eye contact with anyone.

"I'm coming with you," Zoe says as she starts reloading her gun.

"Zoe, I need you to stay with them," I say. "Show them the layout."

"Are you sure?"

"I'm positive. We can handle this." I look over to Fick, who's nodding frantically, and then glance to Vegas, who's slowly shaking his head. As the elevator slows and the door opens on the seventieth floor, Fick, Vegas and I creep out.

I turn to Zoe and tell her, "After you get off, send the elevator back down to this floor. We'll only be a few minutes."

She nods, grabs me by my shirt and pulls me in for a passionate kiss. The door shuts on my head and reopens. It starts to close again as we continue to lock lips.

"Alright, guys!" Vegas says as he pulls me away.

"Come back safe," she whispers as the door closes.

"It's a date!" I say to her, and the elevator shuts completely. I feel as light as a feather. I've kissed a lot of women in my life, but nothing, not even my first kiss, ever compared to the overwhelming feeling that I just had.

"Okay, Romeo, let's go!" Vegas says to pull me back to reality.

"I'm in love, guys!"

"We know. Do you think we can get through this floor alive before you start planning your family?"

"Right, let's keep it quiet. I recall seeing survivors in the east wing. Let's make our way there. Let's go into stealth mode; quiet kills only."

Vegas nods in agreement and holsters his gun. Fickle doesn't have anything anyway, so he just tiptoes along. We come to an open conference room and notice movement. Dropping to our knees to investigate, we crawl by the executives' posh, windowed conference room. Almost immediately, we notice three zombies wearing thousand-dollar suits and shambling about the room like mindless sleepwalkers. We've nearly crept by, trying not to catch their lifeless gaze, when Fickle stops dead in his tracks. Suddenly, he stands upright and stares at one of the suits ricocheting away from the corner of the room.

"Hey," he whispers, "isn't that…"

CHAPTER 28
ALL CAUGHT UP

I DON'T THINK I'VE sat down since this nightmare unfolded. Sitting in this conference room feels nice, with its high back chairs and my feet up on the granite table. Also, finding some cigarettes is a bonus. I don't smoke, but hey, I'm banking that lung cancer won't be what kills me, at this point. While puffing on a cigarette, I drop my feet from the table and lean down.

"So you see, Mr. Grand, that's how we ended up on the seventieth floor, and how you, sir, ended up all busted up, with a golf putter up your ass."

On the floor, a squirming Gerry Grand tries his damnedest to take a bite out of me.

"Fickle did such a number on you, man," I say. With his arms and legs shattered, there isn't much he can do other than moan and snap his teeth. "So, now you're all caught up!"

Fickle and Vegas walk back into the conference room, having checked the final area for survivors.

"We couldn't find anyone," Fickle says. "We should get back to the penthouse."

Suddenly, Fick is walking taller, feeling more confident about himself. Perhaps it's poetic justice that he waited to truly pop his cherry on Grand. That guy was such an asshole to him that it allowed him to harness his inner rage.

"Sure thing, Fick!" I say as I bend down to put out my cigarette on Gerry Grand's forehead. "See ya, asshole!"

Just as I stand up, we all hear a noise coming from one of the tall cabinets in the room.

"Did you hear that?" Vegas asks. We creep over to the cabinet; I'm armed with my paper cutter, Vegas with his table leg. I reach out and grab the cabinet door, opening it swiftly, ready to step back and pulverize whatever's in there. It's none other than a very terrified Kyle Thompson, the guy who Fick lost the CTO job to.

"Kyle! You okay, man?" Fickle asks.

"Fi-Fi-Fickle… Is that you? Oh my god, thank you!"

As Kyle lunges out of the cabinet and breaks down in his arms, Fickle isn't sure how to react. He takes a moment to hug him back, but then, in a sudden move, pushes him away.

"Dude, did you shit your pants?"

"You don't understand! Everyone just started eating each other. I've been hiding in that cabinet for the entire day. It was terrifying!" Kyle cries as he once again lunges forward into Fick's arms. Fickle looks over to Vegas and I, searching for help.

"Hey, man, you wanted to save people. Here you go!" I laugh. We make our way to Zook's elevator, Kyle leaning his head on Fick's shoulder.

"Man, I can't believe you lost a promotion to this guy!" Vegas states with a tone of disappointment.

"Screw you, man!" wails Kyle. "You have no idea what I've been through!"

"Yeah, no idea!" I quip back as I swipe for the elevator doors to open. They don't. It doesn't look like Zoe sent it back down like she was supposed to. As we wait in the hall, I swipe again. Nothing.

"Oh my god!" Kyle screams, huddling behind Fickle. There are five zombies making their way towards us.

"Stay quiet and calm, man," I whisper to Kyle. "Being loud only attracts more."

Kyle tries to cover the ridiculous whine coming out of his mouth. This shit-smelling, sniffling idiot is going to get us killed. And why didn't Zoe send down the elevator? I hope she's not in trouble! I'm now swiping the card frantically, trying to call the elevator while they get ever closer.

"Okay, Vegas. Let's do this!"

We pull out our guns and start shooting. As I pull the trigger and watch each head explode in front of me, I'm overwhelmed by the smell of gunpowder, blood, brain fragments and the shit in Kyle's pants. As they drop in front of us, more start to come out of the woodwork. We're quickly getting overwhelmed by zombies! I run out of bullets and throw my gun to the ground, pulling out my shredder. It's not long before Vegas is also out. We frantically slash and pummel zombie after zombie, creating a shower of blood and gore. Kyle is now sucking his thumb, rocking against the door of the elevator, but Fick is doing his best to keep the zombies at bay. Suddenly, the doors open, and we jump in, slashing and hacking as they close.

"Damn, that was close!" I say as I wipe the blood from my blade and my face. Kyle is crying like a baby on the floor, but over the sound of his sobbing, I hear something familiar.

"Shh, you guys hear that?" I ask. Kyle is still blubbering like an idiot. "Kyle, shut the hell up!"

"What is it, Tyson?" Fick responds.

"Listen!"

Everyone sits quietly for a few seconds. Even Kyle is holding his breath to listen to what's up. As silence falls through the elevator, you can hear the muzak come through. It's Michael Jackson's *Thriller*!

"Do you hear it? This is *Thriller*!"

We all break into our best *Thriller* dances. Well, except for

Kyle, who after watching us mow down and chop up two dozen zombies, probably thinks we're insane. Dancing and laughing, we make our way back up to the penthouse to make our escape.

The elevator doors open on the penthouse and I fly out to find Zoe. She greets me just as frantically.

"What happened?" I ask. "I thought you were going to send down the elevator?"

"I know, and I did, but Derek and Dylan saw a couple of people on the security monitors and wanted to help. He felt terrible about how he acted and wanted to see what he could do. He's down on the sixty-third floor right now, and he and Dylan are on the run."

"Okay, Vegas, go to the monitor and get a good idea of where they are! Fick, come here and turn on your video."

Fick reaches down to turn on his camera.

"Uh oh, my battery is really low. Better make this message count!"

Fick turns on the camera and points to me as if to say 'action'.

"Alright, everyone, listen up!" I say, taking my cue. "We're alive and well, for the most part. We've found some survivors, and we're getting a few more. We hope to save as many New Yorkers as possible, but there aren't many left. We're ready to get out of here any time now. Pray for us!" I nod to Fick and he shuts the camera off. "Okay, hopefully our ride is on its way. We need a few of us to stay here and hold the 'copter while we get the others! Fick, you stay here with Kyle. Zoe, Vegas and I will get Derek and Dylan!"

Fick looks desperate to go with us and tries to walk towards me, but Kyle is holding his leg.

"Please stay with me!" he begs. "I'm so scared!"

Fickle reluctantly agrees.

"Vegas," I say, "you have an idea where they are?"

"Yep, but you're not going to like it!"

I'm morbidly curious what could possibly be worse than what we've already been through.

"Tell me!"

"They're trapped in the gym area by a bunch of huge, muscle-man zombies!"

I pause for a second, trying to digest what Vegas just told me. Apart from Fickle, who's still being restrained by Kyle, we all run towards the security monitors. Sure enough, there are a half-dozen 'roided-up zombies beating on a door we don't have camera access beyond.

"I'm pretty sure they're locked in the girls' locker room," Vegas says.

"This should be interesting," I say. "Let's go!"

We run to the elevator, intending to travel down to the sixty-third. I'm hoping this is our last run; I'm not sure I can take much more. I'm exhausted! The elevator door opens, and we all climb in.

"We'll be back, Fick. Don't let the 'copter leave without us!"

Fickle nods as he finally escapes the clutches of Kyle.

"Come back soon, guys!"

Sitting in the bar, watching the news unfold, Jeffords finally sees Tyson give the signal he's being waiting for. He pulls out his phone and sends the text message: 'You're up. Stick with the plan and godspeed!' He places his phone back in his pocket, drops some money on the bar and makes his way to the exit.

"You going to Zook Towers?" asks the bartender.

"No, I'm heading to Saint Patrick's Cathedral."

"What's going on there?"

"I think I need to talk to God, right now. Thanks for the drink, and be safe!"

"You too, partner."

CHAPTER 29
SURVIVORS

E EXIT THE elevator and make our way to the gym. I've only been here a few times, and I never exercised; I just walked around with a water bottle and a small towel. I stacked weights on and off the bar a few times, but I never actually lifted anything, mainly because I never really fit in. The gym was typically filled with huge dudes and pretty people. There was always a lot of grunting and high-fiving from the steroid meathead types, and lots of sweaty, physically fit people spinning or doing pilates. We creep in and see the beefheads banging on the door of the ladies' locker room. I think if we quietly make our way behind them, we can take care of business pretty quickly. I motion to Zoe and Vegas to follow my lead. They nod, and we slowly approach. These zombies are Hulk-size. I didn't think I could ever see anything more terrifying than a zombie, but now I have a new fear, and it's meathead zombies. I wonder what you call these things: mombies or zeatheads? I'm leaning towards zeathead, it has a nice ring to it. As I take a step, precariously trying to go unnoticed, I accidentally kick a barbell, which rolls quietly across the floor. We all stare at it in hopes that it'll stop nicely and without a sound. No such luck, as it clanks against a stack of forty-five-pound plates. The sound isn't loud, but it may as well have been an airhorn in this otherwise quiet gym. One of the zeatheads stops scratching on the door and slowly turns his head. We stand motionless as he moves his gargantuan head around the room, scanning for lifeforms. He looks at us, but we stay still and he doesn't make us out to be something he wants to sink his teeth into. He turns back to the door and goes back to banging and scratching with his Jolly Green Giant friends. Whew, that was close. I make quick eye contact with Zoe and Vegas, and we all breathe a quick sigh of relief. Slowly, quietly, I pull out my shredder. This weapon has never let me down, and now that I've leveled up to expert, it's time to go beast mode on these zeatheads. Vegas pulls out his crude device as well; guns aren't the best choice here. We don't know how many zombies are around at this point, so stealth kills are the way to go. Zoe, of course, is armed to the teeth, but all guns. She acknowledges our choice of weapon, holsters her gun, bends down and grabs a straight bar from the floor. There are five of these guys, but I'm feeling particularly badass right now, so as we approach, my fear is diminishing. There are three of us and five of them; we've obviously faced worse odds. After surviving the lobby, this should be a piece of cake. We're mere feet from them, now. We're spread out, me in the center, Zoe on the right and Vegas on the left. We all glance at each other, and I can see the anxiousness in Vegas. He lifts his table leg over his head and lands a huge blow on one of their heads. His spectacular bash appears to have no effect on the giant. The zeathead slowly turns, and Vegas' face goes from 'badass' to 'oh shit' in a matter of seconds. The rest of the zeatheads turn, and I quickly go from 'beast mode' to 'WTF' as well. The one closest to me is about 6'3" and two hundred and forty pounds of solid muscle. As he snarls, I muster up enough aggression to slam the shredder into the top of his skull. He takes a few steps back, which causes me to lose my grip. Recovering, he shakes his head, and with my shredder still wedged in deep, he refocuses on me. With a yell, he stumbles in my direction.

"Oh, shit!" Vegas yells, and we find ourselves quickly retreating into the gym, bobbing and weaving between the equipment.

I make my way upstairs to the cardio equipment. This is a dead end, I'm screwed. As he gains on me, I make a beeline for the line of treadmills. I duck under, moving to the other side, and quickly notice that he can't figure out how to get past the obstacle to reach me. He's literally stuck on the treadmill, reaching for me. I stop in my tracks to try and get the shredder back, but this ogre's arms have a lot of reach. As he lunges frantically, I try to time his movements to get my weapon back. We look like we're doing a choreographed dance. In the chaos of swipes, along with ducks and dives, he inadvertently turns on the treadmill. I'm taken aback in amazement, as this zombie is now jogging in place, trying to catch me. It would be hysterical if it wasn't so terrifying. As he struggles with the increasing speed, he starts to pump his arms to run in a full sprint. I take the opportunity to grab the shredder and pry it out of his head. He falls down, and the treadmill's momentum throws him off the back like a slingshot. I quickly duck under and allow the treadmill to propel me in his direction, as I wind up for my kill shot. As he stands, I'm flying into him at full speed, swinging into the side of his neck. As blood splatters across my face and half the room, I realize I didn't make it all the way through. I pull the shredder back for another swing, and the zeathead stands up straight. He looks at me and takes a step in my direction. As he does, his head folds over sideways, causing more splatter to shoot out from his neck. Holy shit! This is the most warped thing I've seen yet. As he takes another step, he collapses at my feet, motionless. Time to check on my friends.

I quickly run down the stairs to see Zoe slamming a twenty-five-pound plate into the head of one zombie, while Vegas is running in circles around a weight bench to get away from two others. There's a motionless one on the floor with a straight bar protruding out of his eye. Zoe's work, no doubt. I make my way to Vegas, since he's the one in trouble. These guys are clearly hardheaded, so I try a different approach. As I run up on Vegas, I swing low on one of the monsters, putting a good slice in his right leg, which causes him to collapse. As he falls, I take swipes into his skull until he's motionless on the ground. As I look up, I see the last beast barreling down on me. I have no room to retreat and no time to pull back my weapon. I'm toast. Just then, a single shot between the eyes drops him at my feet. I look over, and Zoe is holding up her pistol from across the room. She smiles and winks at me. God, I love her. We regroup at the bathroom door.

"Okay, I'm not sure what we're going to find in here. Zoe, I know Derek is your friend, so please brace yourself for the worst."

"How can it get any worse than this?" she asks.

"Never say never," I reply, carefully opening the door. We walk in slowly, but on first glance, there's nothing noteworthy. As we make our way into the locker room, we can hear some commotion in the back.

"It's coming from the shower area," Vegas murmurs. Again trying to be as stealthy as possible, we gingerly step closer to the familiar sounds of zombies feasting. We turn the corner into the shower room hoping, praying, to find our friends alive, but also expecting the worst-case scenario. We peek into the room and see five completely naked zombie women, their faces and chests covered in blood and torn flesh. Apparently, they were showering in the locker room when the outbreak happened. Three of them are crouched over Dylan, devouring his neck and stomach, ripping his tissue and intestines away from his motionless body. The others are desperately trying to tug down Derek, who is clinging onto the top of the shower stall for dear life.

"I was wrong, it *can* get worse," Zoe whispers.

"A little help!" Derek screams from the rafters. We don't mess around this time; we all pull out our guns and lead starts flying. In honor of Dylan, we needed to make quick work of these zombies. In a few seconds, it's over, and Derek makes his way down from the stalls.

"Man, I owe you guys! Thanks for coming for us."

"What happened?" Zoe responds.

"Well, we were thinking about what you guys said about saving as many people as possible, and we agreed we needed to do our best to help as many as we could. We found some survivors but got pinned down in here. Once we came across these zombies, Dylan and I did our best to hold them at bay while the others made it to safety. Dylan put his life on the line for me and the others. He's a true hero."

"Others?" I say inquisitively. Derek makes his way to a supply closet in the back of the shower room. He opens it, and inside are four women and two men, who look very shaken.

"We saw them hiding out on this floor, but we got cornered trying to get back to the elevator. We took refuge in the ladies' locker room, which turned out to be a deadly mistake," Derek says, his voice trailing somberly.

"It's okay, you can come out. It's safe now," I say to the group hiding in the closet. They step out as I walk over. "Hey guys, I know you're scared, and you've probably been through a lot. We have a plan to get you out of here, but we have to move now. You guys ready to move?" They all look exhausted but nod in agreement. "Okay, good. Follow us and stay close. We're heading up to Zook's penthouse."

I look over to Derek, Zoe and Vegas and give them the nod to move. We all get back into formation and make our way out of the locker room, through the gym and onto Zook's elevator. With a quick swipe, the doors open and we're on our way back to the top floor, where hopefully a helicopter will be waiting.

CHAPTER 30
THE GREAT ESCAPE

AS WE EXIT the elevator into Zook's penthouse, Fick and Kyle are there to greet us. Kyle is still clamoring to his hero for saving his life, while Fickle seems annoyed by his new puppy dog.

"We scoured the video footage of every single floor, and there's no one left," says a disappointed Fickle.

"I can't believe everyone in this building is dead," Vegas responds.

"It's no joke, what Zook was working on," Zoe states. "He is the epitome of evil!"

Just then, we hear the noise we've been waiting for; the sound of a helicopter approaching Zook's helipad.

"Oh my god!" Kyle exclaims, darting out to wave the 'copter in. "We're really getting out of here!"

Everyone else breaks out into celebration. I'm taken aback by the sheer luck of it all. I can't believe a handful of computer nerds actually navigated their way through a zombie-infested building, outsmarting and outmaneuvering all others to escape. I lean back on Zook's fifteen-thousand-dollar couch to take it all in.

"Hey, man," Derek says, dragging me out of my thoughts. "I

didn't get a chance to thank you for saving my life back there. It took a lot of guts to come after us like that."

"I could think of a few worse ways to die than getting your face chewed off by a bunch of naked women," I reply, "but only a few."

He chuckles a bit before leaning in and saying, "Also, I want to let you know that Zoe and I are just friends. All that other stuff; I was just screwing with you."

"I appreciate that."

"She really likes you, I can tell. I tried to get her to look at me the way she looks at you, but I couldn't get it to happen."

We both stare at Zoe until it becomes uncomfortable for everyone, including Zoe, who's now looking at us inquisitively. We laugh and bump fists.

"Now, I better go get that dumbass off the landing spot so the helicopter can actually land," Derek says before jogging outside.

Zoe sidles over and asks, "What was all that about?"

"Not much," I say. "He was just telling me how grateful he was to have me save his life, and that he wishes one day to be half the man I am."

Zoe smiles, leans next to me on the couch and puts her head on my shoulder. I respond by putting my arm around her. I reflect on how our day started in the lobby, with me stepping off the elevator, wishing to have my first date with her. What a crazy series of events that's brought us to this moment. As we intertwine on the couch, Fickle and Vegas approach.

"Well man, you did it! You saved our lives," Vegas says.

"*We* did it," I reply, "we *all* did it. You too, Fickle. We wouldn't be here without your help, and your new best-friend-slash-stalker Kyle owes his life to you."

We all chuckle as we turn to see the helicopter coming to a firm landing on the helipad outside. As we take our last few moments inside the penthouse, we see Kyle frantically waving at the helicopter pilot, while Derek directs him and the six other survivors into the copter. Derek motions for us to join them outside.

"Well, I guess this is it. Time to leave the comforts of Zook Towers," I say, as we walk to the balcony. Fickle leads the way, but pauses for a moment to look up at the sky just outside the window.

"What's wrong, Fick?" I holler as I grab Zoe's hand, escorting her to her chariot.

"Wait," Fickle says as he holds his hand up in a fist. We all stop dead.

"Something's wrong." He looks again before screaming, "Incoming! Everyone down!" He turns in our direction and pushes us all away from the balcony. Suddenly, a flash lights up the balcony, followed by a huge explosion. The windows blow out a second before the shockwave knocks us all to the ground. As I try to get up, I'm pushed back by the extreme heat, and I hold up my hand to cover my face. I try to make out what happened, even as I realize it doesn't matter. I quickly change gears. It's not what happened; it's what's left. The helicopter has been completely obliterated, along with everyone who was outside.

*

Sergeant Major Braxton Reflects

Outside Zook Towers, sitting in my temporary barracks in complete solitude, I contemplate the magnitude of what I have just done. In wartime, these decisions are easy. We evaluate the threat and we take it out. There isn't much to think about or reflect on, except strategy. On American soil, the playbook is the same, but the emotional price is much higher. It's not lost on me that an explosion on a skyscraper in New York city is sure to evoke fears and memories of one of America's darkest days. It's not something

I take lightly. Still, I know what I did was strategically right. I know I had to contain the threat. The risk of this virus leaving the quarantine zone was too high to gamble on. Still, they were Americans simply trying to survive. Based on the behavior of this virus, I know the likelihood is they weren't infected. However, there was still a risk, and I had to act on that, for the greater good. Prior to the explosion, the growing crowd outside was deafening and difficult to contain. Now, I can hear nothing; no one is screaming, only silence. Perhaps they too are evaluating the magnitude of what just happened and coming to terms with the inevitable fate of victims trapped in a no-win situation. Or maybe this city is locked in fear by the ball of fire in the sky. No terrorist; this time, it came from me. Perhaps, later, they'll choose not to judge me, but to respect the difficult decision I made in order to protect them. Perhaps they'll come to villainize me for my actions. Either way, what's done is done. I can only reflect. Did I do what's right, or did I do the right thing? Sometimes, the two don't go hand in hand.

*

As the heat subsides and the smoke clears, I quickly assess the situation.

"Everyone okay?" I scream out.

"I'm okay," says Fick.

"Present!" calls Vegas.

"Zoe! Zoe?" I shout. "Where are you?"

"I'm here!" she calls out, pushing the couch aside. She stands up and brushes herself off.

"What the hell happened?" I ask, shell-shocked. "They just killed a cop! They killed Kyle and Derek! *Why?*"

"To make sure we never leave this tower," Zoe responds. "We're just as much of a threat as the zombies."

"That doesn't make sense. We're not sick!"

"They don't care. Being in this building means we're a potential threat; they're not prepared to take that risk, no matter how small."

"So, now what? Do we just sit here and die?" I yell. "This is bullshit; we have rights!"

"Rights no longer apply to us."

"Yes, they do!" I chime in. "And we're not done yet! We have another way out."

"Oh, give it up, Tyson!" Vegas responds. "I'm sick and tired of you telling us we'll be fine. The odds are against us here, and we have no more moves! We're in checkmate, so please stop trying to fill our heads with nonsense! Sid, Matt, Frank, Dylan and now Kyle and Derek are all dead, and they all died believing! Give it a rest! We all know how this is going to end."

I understand where Vegas is coming from. We're up here because of me and what I thought was best. To be completely honest, we're only alive because of dumb luck and help from Zoe and her friends. We should have died a long time ago. Still, we *have* come this far, I just need them to come a little farther.

"Listen, Vegas, I get it! We should all be dead. I carry the weight of each of the names you called out. Sid was one of my best friends, and he died sacrificing himself so we could live."

"Well, technically he died because he had sex with an STD-riddled zombie!" Fick chimes in.

"Come on, Fick," I say sternly. "Listen, I know if we get outside this building, we aren't going to die. We just need to show them we're no threat. Now, I'm not ready to give up. We've sacrificed so much, our friends have sacrificed so much. Let's live for them, for their families, so they didn't die in vain. Who's in?"

"I'm in," Zoe says.

"I'm in, too," says Fick. "I'd rather die trying to live than just waiting to die."

"Come on, Vegas. We've come so far, let's finish this!"

"Okay, Tyson, what's your plan?"

"Great, time to step it up! Fick, you still have juice for your phone?"

"I don't know, Tyson. Maybe a few seconds left."

"Worth a shot! Okay, turn it on and face me."

Fickle hits the power button and waits for the boot sequence to complete. Once it has, he starts his video recorder. He points to me as if to say 'action'.

"Hello, America! Well, someone tried to kill us, again. I'm assuming it's the military, controlled by Zook to hide his dirty little secret. Well, he missed some of us, but he got the rest and killed an NYPD officer, in the process. Is this the new America? Where we kill each other to protect secrets? Well, I have news for you; we are New Yorkers! We don't die easily, and we never give up. To my fellow citizens: Zook and his friends built a bio-agent in your backyard, and now they're trying to hide it. Rise up! We'll be out of here in a few, and I know you have our backs. To our military friends watching, we're getting out of this building, and we're coming for you. See you soon!"

The phone goes dark.

"That's it, battery dead," Fickle says, pulling the phone off the front of his shirt.

"Well, I think I got my point across."

"I'll say you did," Vegas agrees. "Now, do you mind sharing how the hell we get out of here?"

"First thing's first," I say as I turn to Fickle. "Fick, I know I've been hard on you, and if we're being honest, you could've gotten us killed countless times. That said, you stepped up and saved all of our lives by not letting us step on that balcony. You did it, man. You saved our lives!"

I can see the pride bloom in Fickle as he takes in what I'm saying. He knows it took him a while to comprehend the magnitude of our situation, but he's earned the rank of hero, and he's beaming. He smiles for a few more moments before looking over to me.

"Thanks, Tyson. But now what?"

A coy smile creeps across my face, and I say, "Follow me!"

With everyone in close pursuit, I dart from Zook's penthouse to his boardwalk, which is connected to tower two. As we run across the boardwalk, I notice the huge crowd amassed below. I slow down to a snail's pace to take in the view, and the others quickly follow suit.

"Holy shit!" Vegas exclaims. "There have to be twenty thousand people down there."

He's right; it's quite the scene. Not since New Year's Eve in Times Square have I seen a crowd this big. The people have come out in droves to view the spectacle of Zook Towers. I hope they're all here rooting for us, united against Fredrick J. Zook. Hey, maybe we can use this to our advantage.

"Hey, guys, let's get their attention," I yell to the group.

"We're one hundred stories up. No way they're going to see us," Fickle responds.

"Come on, that sounds like a challenge to me," I say with a smile. We all look at each other for a second and then start jumping and screaming like maniacs, barely visible on top of the Zook Towers 'Z'.

"Up here!"

"Look at me, you assholes!"

"Woohoo!"

Down below, in the reporters' section, Mark Fields stands with fifty other reporters. He's on the phone, talking to his producer, when he glances up to see movement.

"I don't believe it. Put me on in thirty seconds! Just do it!" As he closes his phone, he runs over to his cameraman. "Zoom in on the top of the 'Z' and tell me what you see."

"Holy shit, I see four people jumping up and down like crazy!"

"*Yes!* On me, we're going live. Get ready to pan up there on my cue!"

Mark quickly fixes his hair and turns to the camera, receiving the signal that he's live.

"Hello again. Mark Fields here, now reporting from ground zero of Zook Towers. As you and the rest of the world saw just moments ago, there was a huge explosion on top of tower one which can only be described as a military mission to stop people from escaping the towers. Well, in breaking news that you will only see on this channel, it appears that the military missed its mark. As my cameraman zooms in, you can clearly see four survivors waving frantically to us below." The camera tightens on our jumping figures. "This is an obvious attempt by those still in the building to make contact with us, likely to let us know they are safe and still in desperate need of rescue."

Back up on the boardwalk, we continue to jump around.

"*Hey!*"

"Can you hear us?"

"Guys, I don't think they can hear us, or even see us," I say dejectedly. Just as we lose our enthusiasm, we hear a huge roar from the crowd below.

"Holy shit, they *can* see us!"

This gives us all a rush of adrenaline, and we start hugging and screaming down to the crowd.

"Alright, guys, time to give them something to show we aren't ready to give up," I say with a smile.

Back down on the ground, the camera remains trained on us.

"They appear to be in good spirits, despite the colossal odds against them," says Mark Fields. "As you can see, they're jumping and hugging as if they have… They appear to be gesturing to the crowd here. Oh wait, they're doing something. Let's zoom in a little closer."

It's then that we drop our pants and place our asses on the window of the boardwalk.

"Well, it looks like they're mooning us, right now! Interpret that how you will. This is Mark Fields for *Channel Two News*."

"And you're off!" laughs the cameraman.

"Not quite Pulitzer material, Tyson," Mark says, dropping his microphone to his side. "Thanks a lot."

We all have our asses to the window. To me, this is the biggest middle finger we could possibly give to those trying to kill us. I've never felt more alive. We have zombies that are trying to eat us and the strongest military in the world trying to silence us, yet here we are, with our asses to the window in the ultimate act of defiance. Honestly, I can think of nothing more American, right now. As we all look at each other in our ridiculousness, we hear something familiar from outside the window. We look back to see a military chopper rising up into view. We quickly pull up our pants and start running down the boardwalk. As we clear to tower two, I give the chopper one last middle-finger salute. He gives it back, and then an actual salute and a smile. Perhaps they *are* on our side, after all. Either that or the pilot is a New Yorker. I look down one more time to the massive crowd below. As I do, I notice some movement in the skyway below. I focus to take a closer look. Shit, it's full of zombies! Tower two is not the safe zone we think it is. I look back up at the helicopter hovering outside. He too notices the zombies flooding the skyway. There's no time to spare; I need to warn the others.

In the barracks, Sergeant Major Braxton is on the radio.

"Take the shot."

"Negative," responds the pilot. "There's no clear shot, and the lower skyway is flooded with zombies. Taking a shot could cause a containment issue."

"Dammit!" Braxton responds, throwing the radio against the wall. "Bring me Chief Franklin, right now!"

"Yes, sir."

Moments later, Chief Franklin is escorted in by two MPs.

"Well, Chief, it looks like your friends have made their way to tower two. Anything I should know about that?" Braxton asks.

"You killed my pilot," growls Franklin. "You can go to hell!"

"I'm sorry I had to do that; it's not something I take lightly, but I told you exactly what would happen if you didn't help me. Let's be fair, your pilot would be alive right now if you'd cooperated fully with me from the beginning."

"And there'd be a lot more people alive right now if we worked *together*. This is not a hot military zone, this is New York City! We help people, we don't trap the innocent or kill them if they disobey us. This isn't Iraq or Afghanistan, but you didn't want to listen, you wanted to come in here and put your thumb on the situation. Your ego killed Americans, today! Don't you try to turn this around on me."

"Well, what now?" asks the sergeant major, shaking his head. "Where do we go from here? I've never had anything but the best intentions for all Americans. I needed to contain the situation to protect everyone. I hope you understand that."

"I understand that rules of engagement are easy for you. They're black and white. Well, nothing is black and white here. It's adapting to the climate, the crowd, the situation. Something you're terrible at!"

"Let's work together, then. I don't want to kill anyone else. Do you know what their plan is in tower two?"

"I honestly do not, and if I did, I'm not entirely sure I could trust you, at this point."

"Well, I'm all out of moves that save people, Chief. My next one is to risk my troops' lives by sending them into tower two to eliminate the threat."

"You do what you have to."

"I'm doing my job, Chief! I'd expect someone in your position to understand that!"

"I understand just fine. You took your military playbook and applied it to Americans. When you do that, nobody wins. We all lose!"

Braxton takes in Franklin's last comment, now standing toe-to-toe with the chief. He looks him up and down one more time before spinning one hundred and eighty degrees and walking away.

CHAPTER 31

BREAKING THE LINE

I CATCH UP TO the others waiting at the elevator.

"Guys, it looks like we're not out of the woods just yet. Zombies are flooding over here on the skywalk. We need to be careful."

"Damn, man. Can't we ever catch a break?" Vegas chimes in.

"We should be fine, just as long as the crosswalk we're going to is clear, it's a straight shot."

We make our way down in the elevator and cross the crosswalk of the dark building. So far, all looks clear. As I start to reflect, I'm thankful for my time with Sid, for meeting Matt, Dylan, Frank and Derek. I'm thankful for me and Zoe, that Fick is suddenly beaming with confidence and that my friend Vegas is still with me. We press on and make our way to the final hallway that leads to our way out. It's funny; when Matt was telling me about Zook's paranoia and his secret escape route to the newsstand across the street, I expected a much more sophisticated path. It's actually pretty plain. Even the door itself is nothing more than a bar-push. Pretty low-key for a man that poops in gold-plated toilet bowls. Matt, being as crazy as he was, ultimately had the plan that would save us. I'm so lucky we met. As we close in on the door, we hear a noise coming from the darkness of the hall behind us. We pause for a moment to look back into the darkness, hearing another noise that's slightly louder. Our hearts are beating out of our chests; the room reeks with the smell of our fear. We shuffle backwards, making our way to freedom without taking our focus from the sounds coming from the end of the hall. As we step back, our biggest fear is realized. A small group of zombies make their way into the light. Smelling our fear, they scamper in our direction. We turn and sprint as fast as we can down the long, narrow hallway. As we run, I can't help but wonder if this is the end for us. Have we come all this way, just to be devoured mere feet from our freedom? The door's in sight, but the zombies are closing in!

We can hear the commotion of the crowd outside; we're literally steps away from freedom, or at least a moment of freedom. We know we're risking gunfire as soon as we step outside, but we can't worry about that now. I don't know about the rest of the group, but a bullet in the head sounds like a much better way to go than being eaten alive.

"Okay, guys," I shout, seeing that we're nearly there, "this is it. On the other side of this door is freedom. We surrender from here."

They lower their weapons and I barge through the door. We tumble out of a fake newspaper stand and onto the sidewalk, across from Zook Towers. I leap up, tripping over my own feet, and reach for the door, managing to slam it shut right as sunlight falls across a slobbering face. The door seems secure enough to hold them, but we can't be too sure. As we step back from the door and out into the crowd, it all seems so surreal. We gaze up at the enormous towers surrounded by helicopters and military personnel, taking in the crowd that's still fixated on the building in front of us. In this moment, I feel like I could just slide into anonymity and disappear. I look over at Zoe and smile, as we share a moment that seems to last forever.

We hear a voice in the crowd cry, "It's them!"

Suddenly, we're mobbed by New Yorkers! You would think they'd be apprehensive of getting this close to us after what we've been through, but it doesn't seem to matter to them. Instead, there's a deluge of hugs and high-fives. Funny; I started my day feeling like a celebrity because someone wanted to take my picture as I went into Z Towers, and I'm ending my day a celebrity for having managed to get out.

Unfortunately, the celebration is cut short by several soldiers in hazmat suits. They appear from nowhere, armed with M16s, and circle around us. They quickly have us surrounded, and then we're on our stomachs. As the soldiers lock us down, a figure appears through the tight circle.

"Tyson, I presume? I'm Sergeant Major Braxton. The party is over."

CHAPTER 32
WHERE ARE WE NOW?

BELIEVE IN OUR last communication, I left you with a bunch of soldiers with guns to our heads. Well, you'll be happy to know that it didn't end with us being brutally murdered on the street, nor did the zombies breach quarantine. We spent the next three weeks in military quarantine; better than death, but only slightly. They spent that time poking and prodding us in the worst ways imaginable. I'm guessing that I may have a similar experience if I'm ever abducted by aliens. After we were violated both physically and civilly, we were free to go, and all went on to cash in on our fame.

Mark Fields

Mark Fields never won the Pulitzer, but he did put himself on the map. He ended up starting his own TV show trying to uncover the hidden plots and agendas of dirty politicians. His show was nominated for an Emmy.

Braxton

Braxton was given a medal for his heroic actions at Zook Towers. He declined the medal and resigned from the military. He was never seen or heard from again.

Chief Franklin

Chief Franklin was never charged with obstruction and was given a medal for his and his team's brave service. He gave the medal to the family of the NYPD pilot who lost his life trying to save others on the top of Zook Towers. He's still the chief of police.

Fickle

Fickle opened up a very successful survival camp where he trains everyday people in how to survive a zombie apocalypse. He's also a motivational speaker and life coach for those looking for confidence or a job promotion. He still lives in New York City, and has since married, with a kid on the way.

Vegas

Vegas ended up earning nine million dollars from people betting on our lives. He partnered with a friend to make an online video game called *Escape Zook Towers*. The cool part of the game is that no one has a chance to get out alive if the Tyson character dies. He moved to Las Vegas and gambles every day.

Me and Zoe

As for me and Zoe. Well, after interviewing all the witnesses, law enforcement and anyone else who had a different perspective on Zook Towers, I wrote a book about the entire incident which you are reading now. Zoe and I went on a short book-signing and talk-show tour. After a few months, our celebrity faded, and we tried to settle back down in New York. It just didn't feel right. Paying homage to one of Z Towers' victims, we decided to sell all of our belongings, and will spend the next six months hiking the entire Appalachian Trail. I guess this is our happily ever after.

Almost Forgot

You're probably wondering about Zook and Jacobs. Well, that story doesn't end well. Shortly after the Zook Towers were contained and cleared of zombies, the investigation quickly shifted to Zook and Jacobs. Military personnel moved in on Zook's estate. They broke into the house and found Zook in one of the rooms, completely zombied out (thanks to Jacobs, no doubt). Zook lunged at the soldiers and was shot and killed. A fitting end to his legacy. He was a figurative monster in life and a literal monster in death.

After combing through the estate, there was no sign of Jacobs and, more disturbingly, no sign of the bio-agent that was stolen from Zook Towers. The only clue found was the phrase 'The End Is Near, Genesis 6:13!' carved into the wall of the room where they found Zook. For all the greatness that Zook thought would be his legacy, he won't be remembered as the greatest American patriot, but as a weak, small man with stunted feet, who risked the lives of all Americans due to his greed for power and infamy. Thanks to his ego, hatred for others and lack of any actual intelligence, America and the rest of the world is, and will always be, on the brink of an apocalypse. No matter how warped Zook was, I believe that, in his sick mind, he thought he was helping the world. In the end, he was just a pawn in Jacobs' master plan. That monster is still out there, and no one knows a thing about him: who he works for, why he did this or what he plans to do next. Jacobs was last seen walking away from Zook's estate just hours before it was raided. In his hand, a briefcase.

Turns out, evil isn't just created, it's manufactured in the good ol' USA. God help us all!

www.ingramcontent.com/pod-product-compliance
Lightning Source LLC
Chambersburg PA
CBHW032139170626
46808CB00006B/2298